# BRINDERBROOK SPIES

Nikita Santos

ISBN 9798847751988
Kindle Direct Publishing
Paperback Edition

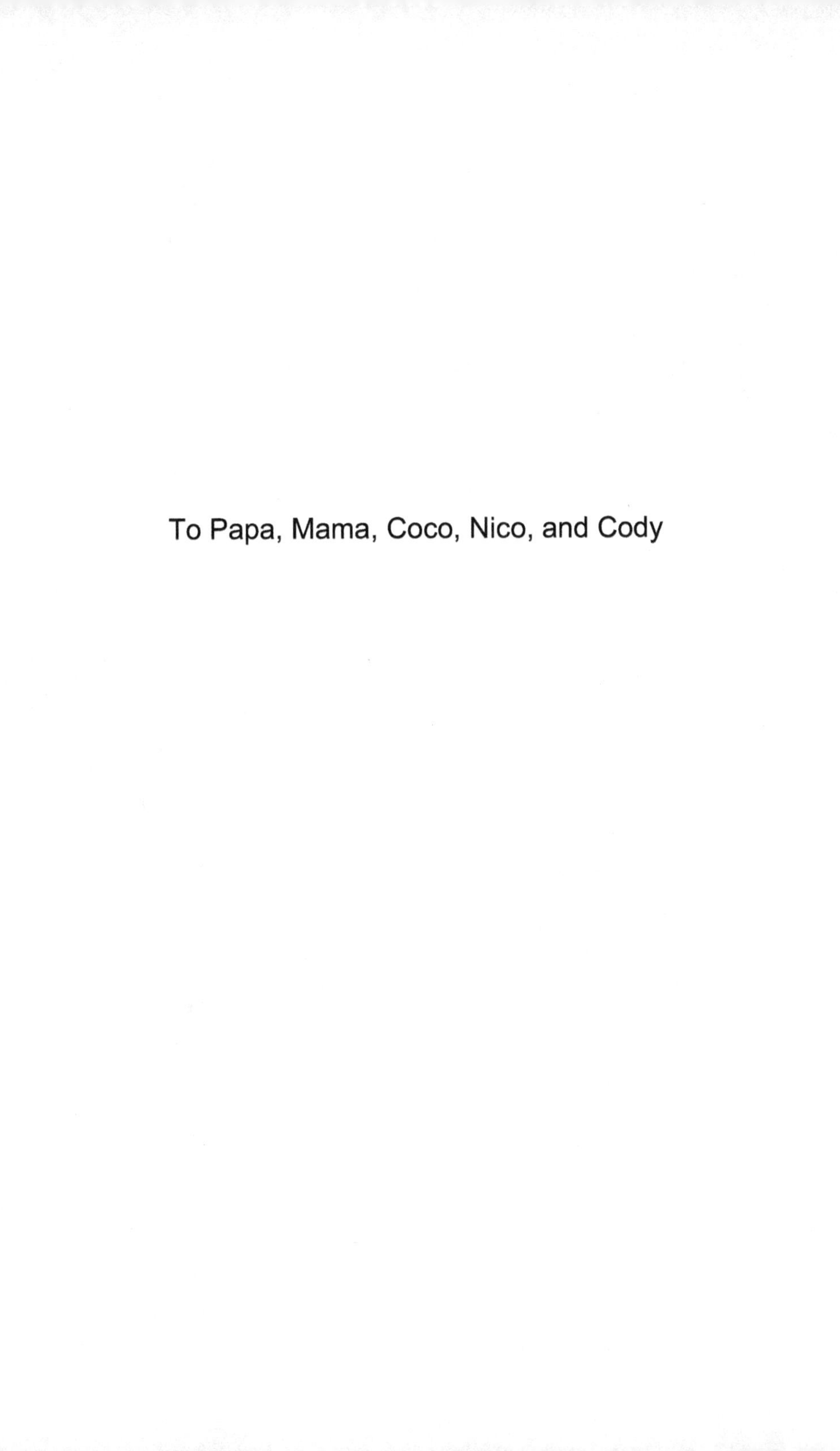

To Papa, Mama, Coco, Nico, and Cody

# CHAPTER 1
## SPIES

On a cloudy day one morning, two friends, Robert Rockedeer and Leila Sparkle, went to school together. The summer vacation was just a few months away.

Robert was a ten-year-old boy with straight dark brown hair and light brown eyes. He loved doing karate and ninja things, but sometimes would get white in the face when wild animals would chase him, and would grow red when Leila would start to become a chatterbox.

Leila was also ten years old. She had wavy orange-brown hair and cocoa-colored eyes. She loved to research, and whenever she enjoyed something, she wanted to be good at it. She would often get annoyed whenever Robert acted a bit too much like a ninja.

Robert and Leila were both average Grade 5 students who didn't have any special jobs, powers, or pets. They had been friends since nursery, and they did almost everything together, such as going to the church, eating the same food, watching movies, being seatmates at class, going to the park, doing homework, and many more.

It was on the first day of school when Robert and Leila, both around three years old back then, first saw each other at the playground. But when the two entered the classroom, their teacher told them to sit beside each other at the same table. From then on, they talked to each other a lot, so much so that their teacher had to say "sshhhh," swapped lunches, played on the swing and the slide together when school was done, and just about everything best friends would do.

They didn't expect the day to be exciting, for the clouds darkened their city, Brinderbrook City. It stood in Southeast Asia, in the country of Brinderbrook. The trees looked gray and the soil black, while everything was dim and dark and it looked like they were in a horror movie.

The clouds were so thick that it looked like it would rain, but it didn't. Robert looked so glum under the clouds. Leila looked so grumpy that it looked like her eyebrows went straight down to her nose, but it wasn't. None of those things were really happening. Everything just looked so strange under the huge dark clouds.

They quietly walked to their school, Brinderbrook Academy. Robert was looking the gloomiest and Leila the angriest, but they looked joyful once again as they reached the classroom.

Robert and Leila quietly walked to their school, Brinderbrook Academy.

The classroom was a big, bright room filled with the feeling of discovering something new. When they entered, every student was roaring with laughter. It turned out that one of their classmates, Red Genshaw, just told a story. He was the clown of their school.

"Whatcha guys laughing about?" Robert asked.

"Red just—ha ha!—told us a story about—ha ha ha ha ha!—about a cat and an octopus! Ha ha ha ha ha!" One of the classmates answered.

As their teacher, Mr. Ramos entered, the entire class sat down, giggling.

A few hours passed, the sun had risen, and school was dismissed.

***

Secretly, a blonde woman was staring at her CCTV, gazing at the two friends walking home from school and chatting. She was in a dark room, as if the clouds that floated above Robert and Leila a while ago were floating over her. The woman sat on a dark gray chair, beside a golden-haired lady, not looking at the television, but at a book titled *Spy Women*. Then she looked up at the blonde woman.

"Do you think those two could be it? They've got the friendship, you know, and I think the teamwork, too. Oh, and maybe they've got the courage and bravery. I saw them stand up against a bully once, actually. Plus, I can see they're spy material. I saw Robert slip his finger in one of his classmate's pockets without his classmate even noticing. He also breaks into karate moves sometimes. And Leila's got the brains, she literally passed all her tests since Grade 4. She's got the sneakiness too. What do you think?"

"Hmm," the blonde woman muttered. "Maybe..." And both their faces lit up in delight despite the dimness of the room they were in.

***

After school, when Robert went home, he found the television turned on. Suddenly, a woman with long, straight, pony-tailed, blonde hair and a striped T-shirt appeared on the screen. She was with a young lady with gorgeous golden hair and pink clothes.

The golden-haired lady looked vaguely familiar to Robert. The woman on the screen shouted. "Hello! I'm Franchesca Birtwick. Here at my side is Maria

Senabi. You're Robert Rockedeer, right?"

"Um, I don't know if you can hear me, but, yeah," Robert replied.

"Okay, great," Franchesca continued.

"Wow, this is a cool show!" exclaimed Robert.

"It just started, Robert," said Franchesca. "Now let me continue. I made this just for you. No one can see it except for you. But some others are also receiving something like this. You—are—a, are you excited? SPY!"

"Say what? I'm a spy!" he cried eagerly, jumping up and down then stopped abruptly to make sure nobody saw.

"Yes. Maria and I are working for a spy company called Spy Studio. If you want, you can be a part of the spies that study here. So, it's sorta like a school, and instead of science or math, you study the essentials of being a spy. Maria and I will be your teachers, and, just like the others, you'll be a great spy, I'm tellin' you. Plus, you could become a professional one if you're great at it already."

"Oh, and why did you choose me?" Robert asked, listening attentively.

"Oh, right. You see, the Spy Studio has special CCTV cameras that let us see what's going on at the other side of the room when we're somewhere else. They can also see things far away, like when you're in Brinderbrook Academy. We have seen your courage, teamwork, friendliness, and more."

"So, you were spying?" Robert asked.

"*Exactly*."

"Wow," he breathed in awe.

"And I'm assigning you to a very important, well, *something*."

At Leila's house, she received the invitation, too.

Franchesca Birtwick said, "Robert and you would be teammates as spies, and *do* work together well."

Her reaction was the same as Robert's, but her mouth was wide open. Maria Senabi was her most favorite actress, and she acted as the main spy in a movie called "Spy Women." Leila was her *biggest* fan.

But then they both heard Franchesca speak again. "Only if you wanna be a spy. It's your choice. If you do want to, call or text us on Spy Sign, our one and only app. You can come here in the Studio at 5:00 p.m. By the way, only people who are invited to become spies can download the app, so nobody else will. You can find the map to the Studio in Spy Sign. We'll be sending our invitation to you…RIGHT NOW! Oh, after you download it."

After Robert did his homework and finished his project about the sun for Science, he sat down in front of his computer and turned it on. He downloaded the app Franchesca mentioned. Then, the exact moment he turned the app on, her invitation popped out in front of him. It said:

*Dear new spy,*

*I, Franchesca Birtwick, the leader of Spy Studio, invite you to become a secret spy. We will be really pleased if you sign up to this app I made myself. If you do sign up, please go to the Spy Studio at 5:00 tomorrow afternoon. If you are not available, it would be fine, too. Thank you for downloading the app and, again, please sign up!*

*—Franchesca Birtwick*

Robert said, "My, do these people want me to do it." And he did sign up.

The next day, after school, Robert and Leila went to the park. "Leila, yesterday I found a show on my television saying that I'm a *spy* and only I can see that show. The lady was a tiny bit weird. She also said that I'd come to something called"—he lowered his voice—"Spy Studio."

"I saw it, too!" said Leila, a bit loudly, "I saw Maria Senabi! You know I'm her biggest fan. The person called Franchesca Birtwick also added that we'd be teammates! Isn't that awesome? Oh, and I did sign up for Spy Sign."

"Me too," said Robert.

"I'll meet you there later."

"What time again?"

"At five o'clock, remember?"

"Oh, right. See you later."

At 5:00 p.m., they did meet at the Spy Studio. It was a humongous place, which was gray in color and full of things that looked like they were for actual spies, like a rock-climbing wall and even cool spy gadgets. There they saw Franchesca and Maria. "Oh my!" exclaimed Leila, "I'm Leila Sparkle, your biggest fan. May I have your autogra…?"

"Of course. But first we have to inform you of your 'thing to do,'" replied Maria.

"Maria's right, that is, after we train you," informed Franchesca. "And if you ace your training, then we could tell you."

Robert and Leila had their most yearning faces on.

Then Robert interrupted. "Um, how did you know our names, Miss?"

"Oh, ho-ho, yes, your teacher is a spy. We asked him to tell us how you act, so that we'd have a better view, because, you know, you go to school every day," replied Franchesca.

"I did not know it. It's definitely *im*possible," said Leila.

"But it *is* true," Maria noted.

"Anyways," Franchesca declared joyfully. "You guys need to start training!"

To begin, Maria led them to two green monkey bars. "Both of you'll need these for your strength," she told them. "Well, since you're just children, we've made it more fun and easy. You'll be training for a few weeks, *or* days, *or* months, and Franchesca and I will check if you've done well."

"That's going to be a long time before we get to know our, what-do-you-call-it, oh yeah, 'thing-to-do,'" grumbled Robert.

"Don't worry," Maria said comfortingly. "You'll go by just fine."

After both their arms felt tired from hanging and reaching out in the monkey bars, they rested a bit then climbed a 'Climbing Triangle.' It was a large right triangle object with wooden sticks attached to each side. They held onto the sticks while climbing up. Afterwards, they practiced their sneaking skills, how to camouflage in the shadows, and more.

After a few days, Robert climbed the Climbing Triangle for the fifth time that day, but Leila stopped him from finishing because she had something to say. "Robby, we need to talk this thing through," she announced professionally.

"What thing?" Robert asked.

"You'll see," Leila said.

"If you say so," replied Robert.

When the two continued training, Robert was panting so much that Leila said they should have a short break. They sat down on a nearby bench. "So," said Robert. "What is this thing you wanted to tell me?"

"Um," replied Leila. "I'm not really sure if you'd like to hear it. I said we'd talk this through, but I changed my mind. Well, it's got something about the 'thing to do.'"

"Leila, you know that from the first time I went to this terrific place, all I wanted to know was what the thing would be."

"Oh, well, sige, but…"

"Please?"

"Oh, okay. But now I don't feel that excited and much more nervous," Leila finally said. "I overheard Franchesca and Maria talking when I was going home yesterday. And, um, they were saying that we'd have a *mission*." She inhaled and exhaled, and then continued talking. "They said that a very dangerous—I'm not sure if I heard it right—that a very dangerous villain called, um, Insect Man escaped from jail and we have to find him and bring him back."

Robert got excited. "A mission? Okay, I'm in."

"But it might be hard because he's a shapeshifter," Leila said.

"Ooh, hard mission, alright," agreed Robert confidently, "But I'm sure we can do it. I mean, it won't be that hard, right?"

"I'm pretty sure it will," Leila said dramatically. "I'm serious, Robby."

"I *know* that we still *can* do it," Robert declared, making a superhero pose.

So, they continued trying with all their heart and might. They practiced and sneaked and climbed until it was night. The duo went home, not saying a single thing about being spies.

The next day was Saturday, and Robert was thinking that they would plan something for their difficult mission. When he was about to phone Leila, someone else phoned him.

"Hello?" he and Leila asked. Leila was getting called, too.

"Hi, Robert and Leila. This is Franchesca." And she told them almost everything Leila had explained to Robert about their mission. But she added, "You will be going out tomorrow, early in the morning. Insect Man escaped from prison last week, but no one found him. All the police said was that his jail looked perfectly normal, but he wasn't inside. *Obviously*, Insect Man shape-shifted and went out, right? But the police said that they had placed magical protection in that jail, and that the covering had been slightly broken. So that explained it. This first mission is to test your training skills, your spy qualities, what you learned in your training, and if you are fit to become a spy. Oh, and I have just decided tonight that it was the right time to tell you. I watched you guys training earlier, and you've got the hang of it. Got it?"

"Yes," the two chorused, not asking a thing about Insect Man.

Then, when Franchesca stopped calling, Robert talked to Leila. "I have a suggestion, Leila," he said.

"Yeah?" Leila asked.

"Do you want to plan for the mission tomorrow?"

"Let me think… Hmm, yeah, okay. Agreed. We'll be thinking of an amazing plan tomorrow."

"Also, I have a question."

"Go on."

"We don't know who Insect Man is, how he acts, his skills, blah, blah, blah. You get what I mean. And…why didn't we ask?"

"Let me just research. G'night."

The following day, Robert went to Leila's house and walked to her bedroom.

"Hi, Leila," he greeted.

"Kumusta, Robby," Leila responded. She was doing something on her violet notebook.

"I've figured out we're going to need supplies," she said. "They look totally normal, but they're not. Lasers, pranks, and more. Here are yours."

"Thanks," Robert replied. She handed him a laser pen, a ball that could turn into a cage, a black suit which was his spy uniform, and more.

It turned out Leila's notebook was a miniature laptop.

"Oh, and I researched about Insect Man," Leila explained professionally. "The mission might be only quite easy because anything that he shapeshifts into has yellow hair. And he likes turning into an ant. Ant Habit, they say. I also downloaded Villains' Lair on this laptop. I called myself the 'Can't Opener' as a villain. The app explains tons of facts about famous villains. They said that Insect Man is so hated because he always steals the money of many families and banks, tricks people often, hurts people, and, you know, always escapes jail."

"Okay, now you make the plan," she said

"Why me? YOU do it!" roared Robert.

"Nope, YOU will do it."

"No, you!"

"YOU!"

"YOU!"

"Ugh. Sige na nga. Fine." said Leila finally. "Okay, this is the plan. First, we wear the uniforms. Then we sneak into Mrs. Genshaw's garden. If we don't find Insect Man there, we go to the anthills that we can find. If he isn't there, we search the whole Brinderbrook City. Then, if he isn't any…"

"I suddenly thought of something, Leila," said Robert, "What if Insect Man isn't in Brinderbrook? What if he's in another city or country?"

"I haven't thought about that…" Her face suddenly looked anxious. "What if you're right? Oh no. If we fail, I'll never ever become an expert or professional spy. Oh no, oh no!"

"Calm down, Leila. Let's ask Franchesca about this question."

So, they ran to the Spy Studio with Franchesca

waiting in front of the entrance door.

"What took you two so long?" she asked.

"We were planning about the mission," responded Leila.

"We have a question," Robert said.

"Fire away," Franchesca replied.

"Well, what if Insect Man isn't in Brinderbrook?"

"Easy," Franchesca answered, "You travel to the first country you think of that you suppose Insect Man is likely to go to."

"But it would take hours to get there," Leila grumbled.

"Not if you use this." She showed them a tiny airplane that she got from the shelf beside her.

"Once you say a country, you get there in a flash."

"Wow, that will work great for us!" cried Robert.

"Not too much. It doesn't work that right yet. But I'm sure Insect Man is just here in Brinderbrook. Anyways, we're in a city full of businesses and that's what Insect Man likes."

"Okay, it would be easy then," Robert said gratefully.

"Oh, do stop talking now and go start finding," ordered Franchesca.

"Yes, miss," the duo said in unison.

# CHAPTER 2
## THE BEGINNING OF THE FIRST MISSION

They put on their spy uniforms in front of their normal clothes and went running and sneaking outside.

The dark clouds were gone and the sun shone, so it was much easier for them.

"First, Mrs. Genshaw's," said Leila.

"The blonde mom of Red. Wait, people are animals too, right?" Robert questioned.

"Correct."

The two ran and sneaked slyly until they were in the garden of Mrs. Genshaw. It was a wonderful place, full of daisies, roses, tulips, sunflowers, some cactuses, mayanas, and more. The middle wall of the garden was with 'Genshaw' written in calligraphy. The very edge was with a silver statue of the Genshaw family in a fountain. And in the center of the entire garden, a woman was planting some ferns.

"Who's there?" Mrs. Genshaw asked. "Oh! Hi, um, are you actors dressed as costume designers? I have many costumes here if you'd like to use them."

"What do you call this garden?" Robert asked,

ignoring her.

"Um, Garden of Love?" Mrs. Genshaw answered, raising her hands.

"Okay," Leila said mysteriously. "Do you know a dangerous villain called Insect Man?"

"No…"

"Who is your son?"

"I'm pretty freaked out right now, you know that I have a son…"

"Leila," Robert whispered, "I'm pretty sure that this *is* Red's real mother."

"Okay," Leila said, convinced that Mrs. Genshaw was the real Mrs. Genshaw, and the duo ran away.

Mrs. Genshaw continued with the ferns, frightened.

***

Following Leila's plan, the two searched from the garden of Mrs. Genshaw to find an anthill. They looked far and near until Leila found a real anthill.

"Here, Robby!"

She was in front of a small anthill and she was grinning from ear to ear. Robert darted to the anthill and he almost smashed it to pieces, but Leila held him from it.

"Look closely for a sign of yellow hair," Robert murmured.

They stared and looked, but no sign of yellow was seen. Then, just when they were about to find another anthill, a small ant with blonde hair walked out of a hole.

"Hey," said Robert, who noticed it. "Leila, look."

"What? Oh, oh, I see it."

"I found yellow hair!" Robert cried.

Immediately, the ant turned into a blonde-haired man with a black domino mask.

"You will never catch me, sickening spies!" And with that, Insect Man sped away.

"Catch that Insect Man! Or…animal!" Leila screamed.

The duo tried to capture him, but he was too swift for them. They ran in and out of buildings, in parks, on rooftops, climbed trees, and past cars but still, they couldn't catch him.

"Why did you shout? We were so close to catching him and you screamed and he ran away! Now we'll never catch up with him!" Leila complained.

"Don't blame me, Leila! Never mind, we can still find him somewhere else. I believe I can capture him. I promise that I won't stop until we find him," said Robert.

"You're mostly saying 'I.' It should be 'we.' So where do we go now?"

"I say we continue the search."

So, Robert and Leila crept between the buildings without making a sound. They were heading in the direction of footsteps Insect Man left for them. Robert tiptoed like a fierce little ninja. Leila made no noise at all, like a cat prowling around to find some supper.

The two acted as though there were CCTVs all around, and they didn't want to be seen. In fact, there *were* CCTVs everywhere.

Robert and Leila hid in the shadows of the tall buildings. They ran towards the entrance of a shopping mall. No one seemed to take notice of them. The buyers just kept seizing things from the shelves and stacking them on a pile of goods.

"Why would Insect Man lead us here?" asked Robert.

"I think he's *tricking* us, Robert. Everything looks normal and the shoppers don't look harmed. We must go to the Studio," Leila responded wisely.

They went out of the mall and sneaked towards the Spy Studio. Leila said that they would just tell Franchesca that it seemed impossible to get their hands on Insect Man. They crept swiftly and they made sure they weren't seen by anyone.

When they entered, Franchesca and Maria were waiting patiently by the front door.

Maria had an excited look on her face, but Franchesca's smile looked worried. "Did you find him?" she questioned them.

"We found him but weren't able to catch him," they responded, sighing.

"Don't worry," Maria said. "The day is not over yet."

"But the sun's almost setting," Robert said worriedly, glancing at the sky.

The duo removed their spy uniforms that they wore over their clothes, and felt sweat trickle down their backs.

"I call that a villainous escape," Leila said

expertly.

"I think *I'll* make the plan," Robert announced, "First, we sneak outside and search everywhere, every building and house. Second, if he turns into an ant the moment we find him, we catch him and squish him. And third, we—"

"He's too fast, Robby, remember?" Leila reminded him.

"And I don't think killing is a great idea," Franchesca added.

"Then we, uh, we use our weapons. And I'm, um, I'm running out of ideas."

"Then we do what we can," Leila suggested.

"You're right," he agreed.

Before Leila followed Robert outside, she left a pack of strawberries at the front door. She researched once that Insect Man loved strawberries and he'd do anything to get them.

Afterwards, the two friends sped out of the Studio straight to a nearby house and inspected the family playing a board game. They continued searching for Insect Man until they searched every house, building, and almost the entire city, yet Insect Man wasn't anywhere to be found.

Exhausted, the duo went back to the Studio. Franchesca was the only one waving at them from the entrance. Leila looked down in front of the door. The strawberries weren't there anymore. She felt that *this* was the right moment.

"Found him?" Franchesca asked.

Then Robert answered wearily, "No, but we

searched every—"

"Yes we did!" Leila screamed fiercely.

"We found him?" Robert questioned. Leila gave him a nudge on the elbow to put him into action. "Oh, yes, we did," he said.

"What? W-where?" Franchesca asked fearfully.

"Right here, in front of us," Leila said calmly but with a fierce and angry look on her face.

"You sneaky spies!" cried Franchesca angrily in Insect Man's voice, and she shapeshifted into him (or perhaps he shapeshifted back into himself).

Insect Man ran to the Brinderbrook Park, but luckily, Robert and Leila caught up with him. He tried to get away, but Robert used his quick ninja skills to block him. Then Insect Man intended to turn into an ant, but Leila moved towards him and placed her right leg up to stomp. So, Insect Man thought that she would step on him (He didn't really know he was speedy. He just thought this). He turned back to a human and ran, but the duo ran with him.

"When did you turn into Franchesca?" Leila asked angrily.

"When you came back to the Studio!" he responded bitterly.

"Where are Franchesca and Maria?" Robert questioned.

"In my house!"

Everyone stopped running.

Insect Man took out a laser pencil. Pew-pew! He directed it to Robert.

Luckily, Robert seized a ball that turned into a shield. Instead, the laser bounced away from the shield and towards a tree. The tree fell and it almost hit Insect Man, who turned into an ant. But he was too quick and he wasn't squished.

Luckily, Robert seized a ball that turned into a shield.

Leila quickly grabbed a mini whiteboard. She squeezed a button and the whiteboard turned into a cage, trapping Insect Man, who immediately turned into a ginger cat. He tried to shapeshift into an ant, but it was no use. It simply wouldn't work.

"You sickening spies! I'll get you two next time!" Insect Man roared crossly.

Robert and Leila glanced at each other and smiled triumphantly. This was the first mission they ever did as spies in training, and they were able to do it.

Before carrying Insect Man and his cage to the police station, the duo went to his house, which was beside a mango tree. Leila directed Robert to it. She knew where it was because she read it in Villains' Lair. In his house, it looked more like a garage. It was a bit dusty and some tiles of the floor weren't secure. But his bedroom was the tidiest of everything. The bed was made, everything was organized, and then they heard muffled talking coming from under it.

"Franchesca and Maria!" Robert and Leila said together.

They pulled their spy teachers from under the bed and removed the black tape on their mouths. "Oh, thank goodness you came," said Franchesca, "The bottom of the bed made me sweaty and there were lots of…ants." She looked frightened and shuddered.

"You're afraid of ants?" Leila asked.

Franchesca nodded. "Nasty things. They give me creepy-crawlies."

"But they're harmless!" Robert cried.

"Everyone's scared of something." Maria shrugged. "Now let's get serious. You two, did you capture Insect Man?"

"Yes," the duo said.

"Where?" Leila showed them a ginger cat with yellow hair inside a cage. The cat purred angrily and tried to shape-shift back, but it was no use.

"Oh, bravo! Bravo! See? I knew you guys could do it!" Franchesca said happily.

"Hold on a second," said Robert. "How did you know that it was Insect Man, Leila?"

"Yes," Maria said, "How?"

"I just had a hunch," Leila explained. "I left strawberries at the front door because I knew he loved them. I researched about him, you see. And when we came back to the Studio, they were gone. And since Maria wasn't there, it must've been Franchesca who was Insect Man because she has blonde hair."

They brought Insect Man to the police station, and the policemen thanked them gratefully.

"Insect Man is the most difficult villain to catch, but you guys have done it," one of the police said.

After they bid goodbye to Franchesca and Maria, they went home gladly, until they saw a ginger cat. "We give up!" they cried, but they realized it was Leila's pet, Groopshie.

So, the two spies bravely fought villains when they came out. But Leila took it seriously, so they sometimes fought. She just wanted to be a professional.

Robert took it fiercely, so they sometimes got hurt. "Fierce like a ninja," he said.

The next month, Franchesca called them.

"Guys, you have another important mission," she said seriously, "I repeat, another important mission about a special monkey."

# CHAPTER 3

## THE GOLDEN MONKEY

What do we do, miss?" Leila asked excitedly. "Come to the Studio this afternoon and I'll tell you."

"Why not now?" questioned Robert.

"Are there any people with you?"

"No," Robert said.

"A helper is," Leila said. "But I can't go out yet."

"So, just go this afternoon, there are other spies here now."

"Yes, Franchesca," they said.

After a while, they met each other in the Spy Studio. Everyone looked happy. Maria was almost crying tears of joy.

"Long time, no see," she said. And she burst into tears.

"It wasn't a very long time, Maria," said Franchesca, patting her on the back. "Now let me tell you about the mission."

"You're going to Africa by this lion statue," she announced. "You must find the Golden Monkey, an ancient statue. And quickly. The kind of monkey it is can only be found in Brinderbrook, but it was somehow teleported to Africa and nobody knows how. It's very rare here. You can do it starting tomorrow."

"But we have school!" the duo cried.

"You two are going to have a holiday from school," said Franchesca. "It's Marvin Calson's birthday tomorrow. Students have one day off from school. Marvin Calson lived in Brinderbrook City. He was the explorer who traveled to Africa by this statue, and discovered the Golden Monkey. It took him a day to find it. Anyway, don't forget to pack your things for tomorrow. Tell your parents what you'll do. I told both of your parents that you are spies. They seemed very surprised. But that's enough." She clasped her hands together. "You may go."

So that Saturday morning, Robert and Leila went straight to the Spy Studio. Franchesca and Maria were waiting by the front door.

"Earlier than we expected," smiled Franchesca.

"We didn't wanna be late," said Robert.

"When do we leave?" asked Leila.

"Same time as before. Just very close to now and you'll be leaving," Maria replied.

After about a minute, Franchesca checked if they had everything they needed.

"Do you have a tent?"

"Yes."

"Clothes?"

"Yes."

"Map?"

"Yes."

"Phones in case of an emergency or if you want to tell us something?"

"Yup."

"Uniforms?"

"Check."

"Weapons?"

"Yes."

"Do you..."

"Franchesca," said Maria. "I think they're ready."

Franchesca showed them the lion statue. It was gray in color, and it was feasting on an antelope. She shakily handed it to Robert, who got it carefully. "I do *not* want you dropping it or breaking it. It's very precious. It's a family heirloom, and I don't want to lose it," Franchesca whispered.

"We promise that we'll keep it safe no matter what," said Robert.

"Is Marvin Calson your ancestor?" Leila questioned curiously.

"No... But he is my friend's ancestor. Why do you say so?" asked Franchesca.

"You said he used the statue to get to Africa, and you told us that it's a family heirloom," Leila responded.

"The lion was given to my family by my friend's family. And *now* I wonder why they gave it to us. But that's another matter."

"You're a great duo, did you know that?" said Maria. "One smart and one full of action. I and Franchesca are counting on you."

"Now let me explain how the statue works," said Franchesca. "This statue has done great things for Marvin Calson, and it will work good for the both of you, too. First, you have to say 'Bring me to Africa'. It is only for Africa. Any place *in* Africa, to be exact. I didn't give it to you the previous mission because it wasn't in my mind. I was just really focused on the mission. Second, you're in Africa and you start the mission. Voila, as simple as that. By the way, you're going to the African savanna."

Robert and Leila suddenly felt a bit frightened. They looked at each other and seemed to read each other's minds.

"Isn't the African savanna with lions?" asked Leila.

"Oh, that reminds me," said Franchesca. "Maria will be there on the lookout. Don't worry. Maria met real lions *twenty* times when filming Spy Women. She's used to it."

Maria nodded.

Robert, Leila, and Maria held the lion statue and cried, "Bring us to Africa!"

Suddenly, everything began to swirl around faster than the speed of light. They heard a very faint sound of Franchesca saying, "Good luck!"

Robert felt like vomiting. Leila felt dizzy. Maria felt excited. The grasslands of Africa became clearer and clearer every second. They heard the elephants and the giraffes. They felt the warmth of the sun.

They all screamed, "Wahoo!" And they finally fell on the grass with a thud.

Leila whirled around for a few seconds and stopped to sniff the air. She grinned.

Robert laid his hands on the grass. He'd never been to Africa before. He felt as if he was going on an amazing adventure.

Maria lay down on the grass but quickly jumped back up again because she felt something rough. "Aray!" she cried. It was a large rock with something carved on it. The carving looked sort of like a monkey. "What's this?" she asked the two.

They shrugged. Then, Leila tilted her head to the side and it struck her. "I think it's the Golden Monkey," she announced excitedly.

"It must be a clue," said Robert, "But did Marvin Calson leave it there or is someone else going on a mission like ours?"

"If we-don't-know-who is going on a mission to find the Monkey," Leila declared. "Then we must find it first. What if they'll use the monkey for something horrible?"

"Guys," said Maria. "No one is going to get the Monkey."

"But if there is someone," Robert cried. "They won't get ahead of us!"

After wearing their spy uniforms, they swiftly ran to the nearest tree to get shade. "I'll make the tent," said Maria. "You two start finding."

Leila pointed to an elephant.

"Why are you pointing to an elephant?" Robert questioned.

"I'm showing you the direction of where we'll

go. Besides, the clue we found was a rock. And, look down." She pushed Robert's head down. Indeed, a path of aligned rocks was leading all the way to the elephant. "A trail of them. They could be leading to the Golden Monkey."

The spies dashed to the elephant's direction. Maria followed them after the blue tent was finished. Leila led them farther in the grassland. They went to parts of the grassland far and near to their tent, turned over rocks, climbed trees, and pushed some tall grass apart to see what was hidden in between, but the Golden Monkey wasn't anywhere. "Hey, what if it's underground?" suggested Robert.

"Good thinking, Robby!" agreed Leila.

"Maybe there's a passage leading somewhere underground. We have to find it."

"Just a reminder," Leila said. "Africa's big."

Maria disassembled the tent to be brought while they find the monkey. She and the duo started walking and searching for any hole or passage leading below the surface.

"I remember researching about Marvin Calson last night. It said that he built a magical underground cave in Africa. No one knows how or why he did it. Maybe it's keeping the monkey. But nobody knows where it is," Leila explained as they walked.

"You should've told us earlier," Robert sighed.

They continued looking for underground passages until Robert asked Leila and Maria something that caught their attention. "Is it normal for a part of railings to be seen like that?" he asked, open-mouthed as he pointed to stair railings sticking out of a hole underground.

"It's normal for a person living underground," said Leila, not knowing what she was seeing. Then, "YOU FOUND IT, ROBBY!"

"Yes!" cried Maria.

"C'mon! Let's celebrate!" roared Leila over-excitedly.

"It's too early for celebration, Leila," said Maria, "So let's just dance!"

They started dancing joyfully until they heard a roaring sound.

"Uh-oh," they all said.

A lion started chasing them! They sped away as fast as they could and didn't stop until the lion suddenly came to a halt. They caught a glimpse of a woman riding the lion. Her hair was chestnut colored and it looked like it had been slashed by a sword. It was up to her neck and very untidy. She looked as though the lion she was riding clawed her right arm. They squinted and rubbed their eyes to make sure this was really happening. And it was.

"Ivory Lark," she said, she leaned and reached out a hand for them to shake. "Insect Man's best friend and nothing else." And, since no one was shaking her hand, she and the lion began chasing them again!

Robert, Leila, and Maria sprinted away as far as they could, moving their legs rapidly. They hid behind an elephant, panting. Finally, Ivory looked around and couldn't spot them, so she headed in their direction, didn't chase them, but looked straight ahead.

"I can't believe we got away from a lion," said Leila, panting, "A lion can run fifty miles per hour. It's unbelievable we did that."

"I'm pretty sure it's tamed," said Robert. "That woman must've told it to go slower. I didn't even know people ride lions."

Maria wasn't talking. Her hands just turned into fists, and she almost looked as if flames would burst out of her head. "What's wrong?" the two spies asked her.

Robert, Leila, and Maria sprinted away as far as they could.

"*Urgh*!" she cried bitterly. "Ivory is the second hardest villain to catch after Insect Man. She is almost as bad as he is! The way she talked sounded like boasting to me. Plus, she escaped jail, too."

"Then we should capture her like Insect Man," said Robert fiercely. "We've got two missions. Capturing Ivory and getting the Monkey."

"Speaking of the Monkey," said Leila, sighing hard. "We've just ran far and lost the passage."

Everybody groaned.

# *CHAPTER 4*

## Inside the Cave

They walked for a while to where Robert led them, after saying that he thought he remembered where it was. They walked for about a minute and, finally, they saw the same stair railings as before.

The three started walking down the spiral staircase. When they reached the underground cave, they were awed. It was a magical place, filled with crystals and stalactites on the ceilings and a little bit of stalagmites on the floor. The ceiling was high and wide. The walls were oddly smooth and silky, while some of the stones that were supposed to be smooth were peculiarly rough.

In the far center of the cave, there was some sort of a stalagmite table on a thing that looked like a stage. And on top of the table was the Golden Monkey. Robert and Leila ran for the Monkey, but Ivory suddenly appeared out of nowhere and grabbed it. She cackled menacingly and vanished. The duo turned around and yelped. Ivory was in front of them, holding the Monkey in one hand and waving to them with the other. She smiled bitterly and attempted to disappear once more, but Robert took hold of the Monkey and seized it.

The three started walking down the spiral staircase.

"How dare you snatch that thing from me!" she cried hotly.

"I did it because it isn't yours!" Robert roared.

"It's not *yours*!"

"Um…"

"Give…" Ivory said as she dashed to the side. "It…" She jumped over Robert. "BACK!" She slid under his legs and grabbed the Monkey. "Take that," she said, grinning slyly.

"Oh, I can do something better," Leila said,

joining in. "I can research your weaknesses and use them as weapons."

"Ha! Ya think that'll help?" Ivory sped to Leila.

"Leila, DUCK!" yelled Robert at the top of his voice.

Leila dodged past Ivory while typing something on her laptop notebook. "Let's see," she said. "You're afraid of crystals? That's kind of odd. Robert, quick! Try to pull out the nearest crystal and hand it to me!"

"Um, Leila," said Robert anxiously. "I'm not sure this is a very good idea…"

"Why?" cried Leila while trying to block a screaming Ivory.

"It might be her weakness because it has a bad effect on her."

"What do you mean?"

"Well, for one, it could, er, *kill* her?"

"Oh, right. We're just trying to capture her to the police."

"You're trying to capture me?" boomed Ivory.

Instead, she went to Robert and reached for the Monkey, but he moved to the side and Ivory fell flat on the ground. She tried teleporting, but it was no use. Maria pulled a handcuff from her pocket and handed it to the duo. "I think both of you deserve to do this."

Grinning triumphantly, Robert and Leila cuffed Ivory's hands together and high-fived.

"Wait, how do we get back to Brinderbrook?" Robert asked, holding the Monkey.

"Use the lion. Franchesca forgot to tell you that it can bring you to the place you live in," answered

Maria. Leila got the lion statue from her backpack and everyone held it, even Ivory.

"Bring us to Brinderbrook!"

Again, everything began to swirl speedily.

Everyone screamed "Wahoo!" while Ivory roared, "AAAARRGGHH!" And they all fell into the Spy Studio.

"You did it!" Franchesca cried, hopping up and down. Then she pointed to Ivory Lark. "Wait, who's that?"

"Ivory Lark," responded Maria. "Second hardest villain to put into jail and the best friend of Insect Man. Robert and Leila fought her bravely when she was trying to steal the monkey. You should be proud of them."

"Yes," said Ivory. "Be proud of them for handcuffing the best friend of an infamous villain. No, I'm joking. And GET ME OUT OF THIS HANDCUFF!"

"I'm sure they won't let you get out of it when you're in jail," laughed Robert.

"Grrrrrrr…" growled Ivory. "I am a teleporting villain, you know I am."

"But," added Leila, "But they use special powers in the jail so that means *you* can't use *your* powers there."

Ivory stared at them speechlessly.

Franchesca clapped her hands and said seriously, "Now let's get to more important matters."

"Excuse me," interrupted Ivory. "I'm more important than that monkey."

"Correct, Ivory," continued Franchesca. "We'll

be talking about the Monkey. Robert, I can see that you're holding it. Please hand it over to me. Thank you. Now, this Monkey wasn't really a golden statue before. Marvin Calson described that the place he found the Monkey in was also with other monkeys that were colored silver and bronze.

"He explained that he saw a man doing something with a leaf. He said that all the other monkeys were sort of trying to push the Golden Monkey away, but the person trying to freeze them did it successfully.

"The question we're all asking now is why did that man turn the Brinderbrook monkeys into statues? Why didn't he bring them with him? Alas, no one knows. Well, some people think that the man turned the monkeys into statues because he wanted to become wealthy. But no one's sure. But the two of you can, although I have another mission for the two of you, and you must do it next month."

"I've two questions," said Leila. "Does the Monkey have some sort of power? Because Ivory's stealing for something, right? Second, why did Calson get *only* the Golden Monkey?"

"Well, you figure that on your own. It's getting dark. You can call me, Maria, and Robert if you've figured it out. Now let's bring Ivory to jail!"

When they reached the police station, the policemen thanked them once again. Ivory kept kicking and stomping inside the bars.

When they went home, Leila immediately researched her questions and called her fellow spy and spy teachers. "I've got the answers," she said. "The Monkey has the ability to give the owner extra strength. I'm glad we got it from Ivory. Next, Marvin Calson only hid the Golden Monkey because he was in a hurry. He needed to be fast because he heard the footsteps of men approaching."

"Thanks, Leila," said Robert.

The following month, when the sky was clear, the clouds were white, the trees swayed in the breeze, the children played soccer, and the birds sang gorgeous songs that brightened up the mood, Robert and Leila's phones rang, and Franchesca, who was calling, said urgently, "Go here, quick. Quick, quick, quick! It's an emergency..."

"Why is it that every month we have a mission?" Robert asked.

"Be thankful it isn't every day," Franchesca said.

"We're coming," Leila said.

# CHAPTER 5

## A Mountain Mission

**W**hat do we have to do?" Leila asked seriously. "It's very important. Well, when I woke up this morning and checked on Maria, she wasn't there in her house. I went to look all around the city, but the only clue I found was a trail of footsteps leading to Mount Jaikabrook. I scanned the footsteps I found in my Spy Studio Dawn Goggles. According to the SSDG, the footprints were left by another one of Insect Man's buddies, Philippe Gorly-Borly. I tried to follow the prints up the mountain but discovered there were a lot of ants. You know, I'm too frightened to get up there…"

Robert said, "Franchesca, there are ants everywhere."

"I know, so get to the Studio, quick."

When the two spies went into the Spy Studio, it looked a bit different. The normally empty shelves were filled with spy gadgets. The vacant cardboard boxes were overflowing with *more* spy gadgets. And a table just beside Franchesca was stuffed with *a lot more* spy gadgets. Franchesca was even holding a luggage bag with *tons.*

"Franchesca?" Robert and Leila asked. "What are all these spy gadgets?"

"Oh," said Franchesca, putting aside the luggage. "I found them in my house's storage, and I decided to organize them here. It turned out there were much more than I expected."

Franchesca showed them her Dawn Goggles. It revealed fairly large footprints on soil. "How did you know it's Philippe Gorly-Borly?" Leila questioned curiously.

"I just took a picture of it that you see on the Dawn Goggles' screen. It only works at dawn, like what it's called. Usually, if you scan something there, it will tell you who the footsteps, thumb marks, faces, and more belong to. Oh." She picked up two Dawn Goggles from the floor and handed them to the two. "Just in case. Now you can start the mission. I'm sure you know where Mount Jaikabrook is, right?"

"Yes," said Leila and Robert in unison. "Just across the river and beside Maria's house, which is on top of a little hill."

"That's right. Now wear your uniforms and go, go, GO!"

After putting on their black spy uniforms, they bid goodbye to Franchesca and crept outside. Robert was feeling thrilled and excited. It was the first time he ever hiked up a mountain. Leila was planning to research Jaikabrook just to make sure they were safe with their gadgets and their sneakiness.

They looked up. The mountain was

humongous. Leila and Robert started backing up, but Robert shook his head and gave Leila a little nudge. He was a bit frightened by its large height, but he didn't want to leave Maria as Philippe Gorly-Borly's prisoner. "Leila," he said, "It's our first time here. We didn't expect it to be as safe and calm. I mean, maybe it is calm. Trying out new things is great."

Leila agreed that Robert was right. "We can do this."

The friends pulled out some sticky black gecko gloves and climbed up the mountain. They kept ascending Mount Jaikabrook until they reached a large cliff. They decided to take a rest. Leila lay her head on a smooth stone as Robert wiped sweat off his face. Then, as Leila stood up, some people dressed in black came hiking up to the cliff.

"Robby," whispered Leila. "Those people look like robbers."

"Roberts? I'm the only Robert here."

"No, Robby. *Robbers*."

"Robbers? Leila, quick! We need to get away!"

They climbed as fast as they could until the robbers were finally out of sight. They panted and continued the hike. They ascended up the mountain, encountering a lot of snow.

Suddenly, Leila screamed. "Robby, my hands are slipping out of the gecko glove! I think I didn't secure it properly!" she wailed.

"Take my hand!" Robert cried.

"I can't reach it!"

"Take my hand!" Robert cried.

Robert thought quickly for a couple of seconds and pulled out a long thick rope from his super-secret pocket hidden at the back of his uniform and told Leila to hold it. "I'll pull you up!" he shouted.

Leila grunted and reached, and she finally took hold of it, relieved.

Robert hoisted her up and said, "This time, secure your glove the right way, and let's continue climbing up."

Leila put her gecko gloves back on, and they started going up Mount Jaikabrook.

Robert felt sweat dripping down his face, and Leila's arms felt numb.

After about a minute or two, they reached

another cliff, except it was larger. There was even a little cave at the side of it. They went into the cave and yelped. From inside the cave, they saw a huge Brinderbrook bear growling hungrily at them.

"AAAARRRRGGGGHHHH!" they roared.

The bear started chasing them slowly all around the cliff, while they ran round and round until they were back-to-back with the mountain. The bear's breath touched their faces, and they were petrified with fear.

"Let's climb up and not look back until we reach a cliff," said Robert.

"Yes," agreed Leila, "Let's do it."

They backed up a bit more until they couldn't move any longer. Robert turned around and so did Leila. They stuck their gecko gloves on the mountain and ascended Mount Jaikabrook as swiftly as they could. They didn't look back until the growls of the bear weren't audible anymore. They sighed gladly and advanced the mountain a little bit more. Now that they were closer to the top and farther from the ground, the air felt chillier. The clouds were getting nearer, and the duo were approaching a cliff.

"Yes!" they cried gladly.

# CHAPTER 6

## PHILIPPE GORLY-BORLY

They climbed up and finally reached it. It was really frosty. Leila pulled out a jacket from her bag's pocket and gave it to Robert. She got another one and wore it herself.

"Wow," said Robert, "You have a really big pocket."

"Yes. It's Franchesca's," Leila replied.

Now it felt warmer in the jacket. They were able to rest for a bit until they heard a shout saying, "NO!" It sounded like a character from Spy Women.

"Maria!" they cried eagerly.

"Where did the shout come from?" Robert questioned.

"Um, I think it came from…THERE!" Leila said as she pointed to the cliff.

"I can see Maria!" they chorused.

"I saw her first!" Robert cried angrily.

"I did!" Leila exclaimed.

"Forget it," he said. "Let's just go there."

They gripped on the little rocks attached to the mountain and moved to the cliff where they heard

Maria. Both of them stepped on the cliff and heard her crying, "I TOLD YOU NO!"

"Whaddaya think is going on?" Robert asked.

"Don't know," Leila responded.

"And why do you think Insect Man's trying to steal the monkey *and* Maria?"

"I don't know either. But you have a point there."

They tip-toed slyly towards a shadowy figure of a man holding a snowy white puppy in front of a lady tied to a chair. She looked like Maria.

"Maria…" Robert whispered.

"Look here…" Leila muttered.

Maria glanced at them and smiled uneasily. "I'm okay," she mouthed.

They gripped on the little rocks attached to the mountain.

"Who's that?" Robert uttered.

"Philippe Gorly-Borly, Insect Man's friend," she seemed to say.

"What's he doing?" Leila asked.

"Trying to drop my dog from the top of the mountain, obviously," Maria mouthed.

"What's that dog?"

"My adopted pet, but I'm just taking care of it for this week," she whispered.

"Who're you talking to?" Philippe Gorly-Borly said.

"N-No one," Maria murmured bitterly.

"I am really going to drop this puppy down the mountain this time."

"NO!"

"Yes I am!"

"No, you gimme that dog right now, Gorly-Borly."

Maria tried moving forward and did for a few inches. She leaned down and stepped hard on Philippe's left foot while he was looking down the mountain. And she grabbed the puppy. Philippe yelled and rubbed his foot. Maria told Robert and Leila to untie the rope tying her to the chair. When she was freed, she embraced the duo.

"Franchesca told us about what happened," Robert wheezed while Maria's hand squished him.

"Um, that hurts," Leila whispered.

"Sorry," she said, letting go. "Now we need to get out of here. Gorly-Borly is the third hardest villain to capture. We need to bring him to the policemen too."

"Okay," said Leila. "First things first, why do you have a dog here?"

Maria shrugged.

"Now, how'd you get here?"

Maria answered, "I felt myself floating high in the air, but thought it was all just a dream. But when I awoke, I figured it was true."

"Third, why are you so angry with Gorly-Borly even if he'll just drop the dog down?"

"The pup's my pet and who'd be wanting to lose an animal they love? And I'm pet-sitting him, though I'll get him next week. Plus, he's going to *kill* Oliver, which isn't a good thing to do."

"Is Oliver your puppy?" Robert questioned.

"Yup."

"Now," Robert declared. "We need to get outta here."

After Maria and Robert picked up the heavy Philippe, who fainted as they talked, Leila started descending the mountain. But Maria and Robert didn't follow. "We need an easier way to get down, Leila," Robert said.

"Um," Leila thought out loud. "Maria felt like she was floating, right. So..."

Maria responded, "Hey, remember that almost every friend of Insect Man has powers? Maybe Gorly-Borly can fly!"

"Can we just call him PGB?" Robert asked, annoyed. "PGB's kinda cool, though he's not."

"Well, okay," Maria agreed. "So, we can build a

hang glider or ask PGB to fly for us."

"I think asking would be better," Leila decided. "Building a hang glider for all of us would take hours."

Leila climbed back up and assisted them in waking up the fainted Philippe. He didn't budge until Robert screamed, "AAARRRGGGHHH! WAKE UP!"

"Argh, argh!" Philippe cried while lying on the cold mountain floor. "W-w-what happened? Where was I? Oh yes, I'm going to drop this p…pup? Where's the dog?"

Maria patted Oliver's soft, brown, fur. She smiled viciously and said, "We'll ask for a suggestion. You fly us down from this mountain safely, and we leave you right after we do something important."

"Let me think about it. Hmm, okay, as long as you keep your promise. You leave me alone after something important."

"Right."

Philippe Gorly-Borly flew them down the mountain, but instead of doing it safely, it was a rough ride. Once the three spies clambered away from Philippe, they sat down at once because of the bumpiness and dizziness the flight gave them. Philippe grinned menacingly and turned around and trotted away.

"Hey!" Robert yelled. "Don't forget what I said!"

"Oh, yeah," Philippe said crossly. "Nope, sorry!"

"Catch him!" Robert cried bitterly. Philippe ran as the three dashed to him.

As they ran, Maria got some handcuffs from a

pocket and gave it to Leila. Leila, who was closest to Philippe, managed to put it on him and told Robert to lock it up. Robert fastened it and Philippe shrieked. They halted.

"This is important? Man, no it's not! No—it's—NOT!"

Franchesca scrambled to them from the direction of the Spy Studio, breathing hard. She panted and nodded to Robert and Leila. Maria went beside Franchesca and quickly explained what happened. Franchesca bobbed her head up and down in response.

"Now," declared Franchesca, "It's time to go to the police."

Walking away from the station, as the policemen waved to Robert and Leila gratefully, they smiled successfully. The duo strolled joyfully around Brinderbrook Park. After a while, they went home with grins on their faces.

At the same time, Robert and Leila walked into their own homes and found the news turned on. In unison, they slumped themselves onto their couches.

The newsperson announced, "According to Teddy Smart, Brookino explorer in one of Brinderbrook's jungles, reports to us that he discovered a rare ladybug, with about a thousand polka dots, perched on top of a leaf. The following day, though, he went back to the same place because he says that the ladybug doesn't leave its home unless they need to hide for protection and other sorts of things. Anyways, he declared his mission of finding the ladybug as the Lost Ladybug expedition. As Mr. Smart says, 'I would be honored if anyone would want to help me.' This ladybug is the only one of its kind, and we would appreciate it if the next generation would learn about it. Anyone who wants to help just needs to visit Mr. Smart—"

"Hey, Jess," said another. "Let's move on to the weather conditions."

At the same time, Robert and Leila's heads lit up with a brilliant idea. They wanted to help Teddy Smart in his extraordinary expedition. They phoned each other to share the news.

# CHAPTER 7

## THE LOST LADYBUG

"What's so important about a missing ladybug?" Franchesca asked the duo after telling her about their new mission.

Leila explained, "Franchesca, we want the people of the next generation to know about the stuff that happened in their history. In addition, it's rare, and we'd be helping a Brookino explorer."

"Oh, I get it. Yes, you're allowed. But inform your parents before you go to Green Jungle."

"We will," said Robert.

After telling their parents, they met each other at the park. Robert was carrying an indigo backpack and Leila was wearing a small handbag. They looked confusingly at each other's bags.

"How can all your stuff fit into that?" Robert questioned curiously.

"Not everything," Leila replied. "I've only got extra clothes, my comb, and my toothbrush and toothpaste."

"Oh yeah, Leila, how can we brush our teeth in the jungle?"

"Um, maybe Teddy Smart has his own house there?"

"Speaking of Mr. Smart, we should ask him first if we could join his mission."

Afterwards, they rode the Bumpin' Bus to the jungle. Robert felt butterflies in his tummy. He never traveled to a jungle before. He imagined a long, slithery snake wiggling up to him from a tree. On the other hand, Leila started typing on her mini laptop. She decided they better know the creatures and plants living in the jungle, just to make sure.

The bus jolted against the road. The luggage of some passengers thump-a-thump-thumped at the seats. The passengers swayed on their seats. The driver announced that they were almost arriving in the Jungle.

Suddenly, the bus came to a halt. The driver said to everyone, "You have arrived at the Green Jungle. Please bring your luggage along with you and wait for the tour guide—"

But Robert and Leila heard nothing more. They crept into the trees and pushed away a few vines. The tree barks were huge and the grass was terrific. The entire jungle was covered with green and brown that the two friends gaped at the jungle's plants.

Robert looked at the tree beside him and jumped. A monkey was chattering mischievously at them and went onto Robert's shoulder. He stretched out his arm and the monkey scrambled back onto the tree. It swung on the vines until it was out of sight.

"Funny monkeys," Leila giggled.

"C'mon," said Robert. "Oh, we don't know where to find Mr. Smart."

"I've got an idea!" she exclaimed as she pulled out a blank parchment from her handbag. The only thing written was 'Tell me the person you want to find and I will lead you.' "Maria gave it to the both of us, but I was the only one there. I forgot to tell you. Sorry."

"Well, that's great! So how does it work?"

"Here, let me read it to you. 'Tell me the person you want to find and I will lead you.' Maria said it can only work for good guys. I think that's why they didn't give it to us before. Anyway, you tell the map where to find Teddy Smart."

Afterwards, they rode the Bumpin' Bus to the jungle.

"Um, okay. Where can we find Brookino explorer Teddy Smart?"

The map revealed nothing for a while, but when Robert repeated it a little bit louder, letters appeared on it. It said, 'Follow the trail of lines and you will find Teddy Smart.' The letters vanished and transformed into a trail of broken lines. At the beginning of the trail, it showed the duo standing together.

Then, at their front, there was a monkey. The real Robert and Leila looked forward. Smiling naughtily was a *true* monkey. It seemed like it was the one that went on Robert's shoulder. They walked towards it and looked back at the map. A drawing of a lonely kapok tree surrounded by bushes was in front of the monkey. They glanced in front of them and saw a kapok tree all alone with only shrub-like plants for company. They trotted forward with the monkey, who went back to Robert.

"How long will it take to get there?" Robert asked.

A few items more, the map revealed.

Another monkey was following the tree. It made a sort of screech. The monkey on Robert's shoulder jumped eagerly and hopped off his shoulder. It went beside the other monkey, which led them forward. The duo saw a tree in front of them. They looked at the map and saw a tree. Then the drawings and letters in the map disappeared. Instead, a sentence popped out.

**You have reached your destination,** it said.

They saw a grand looking tree house on top of one of the tree's branches. A spiral staircase was surrounding the tree. They decided to climb the staircase and then knocked on Teddy Smart's door. The stair was a bit slippery. The two monkeys slid into the window. Robert and Leila had to hold onto the tree bark because there were no railings.

Robert knocked on the door. No answer. He knocked again. No answer. He knocked twice. There came a rough voice saying, "Who's there?"

"Um, we're citizens of Brinderbrook, sir," said Leila.

An eye appeared in a hole at the door. "I have no idea who the two of you are," said the person.

"Um, we're volunteers to your mission, sir," Robert explained. "We want to help you in finding the lost ladybug."

"Ah, that's good, you can come in but I must test your jungle knowledge."

They went in and gasped. The tree house looked exactly like a jungle. The walls were covered in vines. The floor was green grass. The ceiling was filled with all sorts of hanging plants. There was a table at the side with some bananas in a basket. The bed was made of leaves and the blanket was sewn with banana peels. Beside the bed was a tree in a pot.

"I'm Teddy Smart," said the man.

Robert and Leila looked up, startled. They forgot that they were in his house because of the wonders he had put in.

Teddy Smart was a big, tall man. His face was

very round. He had a deep brown beard and mustache. His hair covered almost his whole face and he wore black glasses. He was wearing a beige t-shirt, beige pants, and a pair of beige boots.

"I'm wondering, sir," Leila asked. "How did you manage to plant all these? How are they not crashing to the ground? Is your tree house strong?"

"I live here, little girl. I planted for many years. And yes, my tree house is strong and stable."

"Um, sir?" Robert questioned. "Did you tell us about a test?"

"Yes I did. Speaking of it, it's time to begin. How old are you?"

"Ten," they chorused.

"That's old enough for you to join the mission. There are only three questions, just to see how good you are in jungles. Okay, number one. What is this poisonous plant and describe it to me."

He held up a plant with tiny, white, and arranged in small umbrella-shaped bunch flowers. The stem had reddish spots and streaks. The leaves were bright green, fern-like, and toothed on the edges. It had a bad smell.

"I know! I know!" Leila cried eagerly. "That's a Poison Hemlock!"

"Yes, correct. Describe it to me."

"When someone touches it, it makes a painful rash or hurts in the eyes if that's where the contact is. It's very toxic to some animals and it is *super* poisonous to people. You can identify it by its tiny white flowers that are formed into an umbrella-shaped group. It has reddish or purple spots and lines. The leaves are bright green."

"Very good. Second, how do you find food in the jungle?"

"Um, ask the monkeys?" Robert responded. "Oh, I know! It depends on where you are. You have to know edible fruits from the ones that aren't. Maybe you *can* ask the monkeys for bananas?"

"Okay. Finally, what do you do if you get lost?"

"Find food," said Leila.

"Build some shelter," Robert replied.

"Get water."

"Make weapons."

"Leila," whispered Robert. "I've got our spy weapons in my bag."

"You're ready," Mr. Smart declared proudly.

Later that afternoon, after eating some bananas, sandwiches that Robert brought, and rice and chicken in a can that Leila brought in her handbag, they went out to start the mission. The two monkeys, which were actually Mr. Smart's pets, followed them down the stairs. The monkey that went on Robert's shoulder, Chip, went on Robert. The other monkey, Dunston, climbed onto Leila's arm. The duo carried the monkeys along.

"I wonder who stole the ladybug," Robert said.

"Maybe Insect Man did," Leila responded.

"Couldn't, he's in jail."

"Um, Ivory or Philippe?"

"They're in jail, too."

"Another friend of Insect Man?"

"Could be. Hey, why don't you research about them?"

"Okay. But I need my notebook."

Robert started opening his bag and handing Leila the notebook, when Mr. Smart interrupted them.

"How can you research in a notebook?" he asked, interested, but also a bit cross.

"I searched through my notes before," Leila lied.

"I thought you meant a sort of computer, because I disagree with gadgets in the jungle..."

Leila turned her notebook so that it was in a horizontal position and started typing. She gasped and whispered into Robert's ear, "Someone named Ted Bart is a friend of Insect Man."

"Could it be..." said Robert.

"It couldn't. He's the one trying to find the ladybug."

"What are you guys doing?" Mr. Smart asked, annoyed.

"Nothing," they said in unison, hiding their hands behind them.

They walked further, encountering a lot of plants and animals.

Unexpectedly, Robert and Leila felt that something wasn't right. They turned around to ask Mr. Smart what the jungle feeling was about, but, to their surprise, he wasn't there. They looked above the trees and below, they looked from left to right, but he wasn't anywhere. They checked if Chip and Dunston were still there, and they were. The duo turned back just to make sure Mr. Smart wasn't left behind.

"Didn't he just ask me how I can research in a notebook?" Leila mentioned. "Plus, he said it angrily. Maybe he saw red because he *is* Ted Bart. Maybe he got mad because, well, Insect Man hates us so much that he could also be angry with us. Maybe Insect Man knows about the weapons that we use. You know how Ivory and Philippe acted to us."

"We haven't got any proof," Robert said miserably. "But you have a point."

"Hmmm, we could find Mr. Smart, or should I say Mr. Bart. We could interview him without the slightest bit of giving him an idea that we suspect him as Ted Bart."

"Okay," Robert agreed. He turned around again to walk forwards, but he came to a halt and gave a gasp of surprise. He couldn't believe his eyes. A majestic little insect was standing on top of a leaf. It was the rare ladybug. It had a lot of tiny polka-dots on its back. Its face was small and cute and it was nibbling on the leaf. The leaf was on top of a hand and it belonged to Mr. Smart.

"Ah, M-Mr. Smart! Um, we were looking for you everywhere!" Robert exclaimed.

"If you said that you searched everywhere then you are not honest. *I* looked everywhere and didn't see you, which means you did *not* look everywhere," said Mr. Smart, irritated. "I have discovered that the ladybug travels to other places, such as *this* spy gadget." He held up a ball shield with 'Spy Gadget' written in Franchesca's handwriting.

Robert and Leila giggled nervously and looked at each other. They both thought the same thing. If Franchesca was in the jungle, what was she doing there? They felt worried. They felt frightened. They felt a bit guilty if they were the reason that led Franchesca into the jungle.

"What's she doing here?" Leila asked anxiously.

"Who?" Mr. Smart questioned.

"Nothing," Robert replied.

"Never mind," Mr. Smart said. "Anyway, you guys weren't finding it. Only I was."

"We *were* walking around the jungle and looking," said Leila.

"See? Only looking. Not for the ladybug."

"We, um…," she started.

"We wanted to give you an interview!" Robert cried.

"What?" Mr. Smart asked. "Why do you want to do that?"

"We just want to," Leila said mischievously. "Okay, let's start. Robby, my notebook."

# CHAPTER 8

## TEDDY SMART OR TED BART'S INTERVIEW

**R**obert gave Leila the notebook. She needed it because she would research Ted Bart in the mini laptop. Then they would know if he was Ted or not. Robert felt excited about knowing, but he was overwhelmed at the same time because of the idea that Franchesca was there *and* the thought that Ted really was a villain.

Leila thought that this was going to be the chance that she would become an expert spy. After settling down, they began asking Mr. Smart the questions.

"Okay, we'll be putting this pencil beside you," Leila said. She placed a pencil on the floor. It was really a recorder, "We'll put this eraser there, too."

The eraser was a lie detector.

"So," she read what was written on the screen of her laptop. "How would you react to this scenario? You see your friend being brought into jail by two spies."

"This is the worst interview I've ever had. My friend?" He shuddered anxiously. "I'd feel sad that my friend would be there and try to save him."

Robert saw the eraser light up in a red color. He whispered to Leila that it was a lie. Leila nodded her head and continued.

"Please be truthful."

"I am."

"I'll just put this pad of paper here." It really revealed the truth if someone said something dishonestly. "I'll repeat the question again. How would you react if your friend is brought to jail by spies?"

"I said I'd feel sad and try to help!"

A sentence appeared on the pad paper that Mr. Smart didn't notice (Or Robert thought so). It said, 'He means that he would be angry with the spies but is too afraid to help.' Robert noted that down. He wrote on his own little notebook.


*TEDDY SMART INTERVIEW*

1.   He's too afraid to help Insect Man out of jail and angry with Leila and I.


Leila continued, "Now, what is your greatest strength?"

"Living in the jungle, of course."

Robert looked at the eraser. It lit up green. The pad paper said, 'TRUTHFUL ANSWER.'

He wrote it down in his notebook.

"Third, what's your greatest weakness?"

"I, uh, I… I hate poisonous plants."

Robert looked at the eraser. It glowed red. The pad paper showed, 'He means that his weakness is trying to be a good friend to Insect Man and the others.' Robert wrote that down and felt a bit sorry for Teddy, or Ted. He shook his head. *He's a villain*, he thought, *He's evil. Stop thinking that, Robert.*

"Fourth, why did you choose to live in the jungle?" Leila asked.

"Because, um… I learned about it and decided to travel there. Then I said that it was a wonderful place and lived in it."

"This is the worst interview I've ever had."

Robert glanced at the pad paper. It said, 'He

lives in the jungle to escape Insect Man because Insect Man sometimes treats him like a slave.' Robert noted that down.

"And finally, and most importantly," Leila said as she swallowed. "Who are your friends?"

"There are a lot of them, such as, um, Kenyon, Ivory, Sam, Phil, I can't tell you all of them."

*Wait a sec*, Robert thought excitedly. *Ivory? Phil or Philippe? But who's Kenyon and Sam?*

He looked at the eraser, which glowed bright green, the first time it ever did light up the brightest.

Robert wrote that down. He glanced at Leila, who was staring at the pad paper, open-mouthed.

"Okay, all done," Leila announced eagerly.

She tapped Robert's shoulder and read the notes he took down while their companion gaped at the pad paper. It said on the page:


TEDDY SMART INTERVIEW

1. He's too afraid to help Insect Man out of jail and angry with me and Leila.
2. Greatest Strength: Living in the Jungle.
3. Greatest Weakness: Trying to be a good friend to Insect Man and others.
4. Insect Man treats him like a servant. That's why he lives in the Jungle.
5. Friends are Kenyon, Ivory Philippe, and Sam.

Leila didn't read the entire page. She stopped at number three and exclaimed, "I knew it!"

"I knew it, too," Ted said.

"What did you know?" Robert questioned.

"I knew that both of you are spies and that you are recording this. That pad paper tells the truth and so does the eraser. How did I know? Because I'm always paying attention to my surroundings. What do *you* know?"

"We know that you're a villain," Leila cried proudly. "A friend of the infamous shape-shifter Insect Man. So now go and come close to us so that we can…"

Too late. Before she could finish the sentence, Ted Bart sped away with Dunston and Chip. They headed towards the city. Franchesca faded out of Robert and Leila's minds. They wore their uniforms, ran and tried to catch up with them but, like Insect Man, Ted and the monkeys were too speedy. Although they couldn't keep up, they reached Brinderbrook Street. Robert turned left and Leila turned right, but Ted and the monkeys weren't on the street nor inside a building. Leila turned front and Robert turned to the jungle but still, they were nowhere.

They faced back-to-back and Robert said, "Let's split up."

"Okay," Leila agreed.

# *CHAPTER 9*
## TED BART'S CHASE

obert headed to the Spy Studio's path while Leila to one of the hotels. Robert looked around and flipped over some trash cans and big leaves, but the monkeys nor Ted weren't there.

Leila crept into the hotel's shadows. The hotel was huge, gold, and white. A giant chandelier was hanging on the ceiling. Tons of people were walking all over the place. This made it hard for Leila to see if anyone had two pet monkeys and was full of beige clothing. Suddenly, at the same time, they heard a monkey chatter. One sounded like Dunston while the other sounded like Chip. The both of them didn't recognize the sound.

"Who's there?" they asked, alert.

In response, the monkeys chattered and gibbered. Robert and Leila whirled around. No one was there. They faced the other way. No one. They continued tip-toeing around, then the monkeys jumped from behind.

"Oo-oo-ah-ah!" Ted's pets cried.

Robert tried to catch Chip, who was the one

with him.

Leila dodged a banana peel Dunston threw at her.

Robert ran towards Chip. Leila headed to the exit, where Dunston kept throwing the bananas. They dashed to the monkeys, and, very painfully, they bumped into each other.

"Aray!" they exclaimed, rubbing their heads.

"Sorry," Robert said.

Then, unexpectedly, Leila burst out, "Urgh! We can't do this! I'm going out on my own! You go your way and I go mine!"

"What just happened?" Robert asked.

Leila didn't answer and stomped off. Robert finally understood. *Leila really* loves *being a spy*, he thought in his head, *she really wants to be an expert. Hmm, maybe she's so mad because our plans aren't working.* Robert just went the opposite direction, becoming a little bit angry with Leila that she likes being a professional more than staying with her friend.

On the other hand, Leila walked down a subway. There was no one there. It was dim and creepy.

She thought, *our plans always work on other missions! What* is *wrong? Oh, I'll figure this out so that Franchesca will announce that I'm a professional.*

She got a bonnet that was hidden inside her leggings. The bonnet had a flashlight in the middle. She wore it on her head and flipped the switch of the flashlight to turn on the light. Immediately, the light flashed on. She saw a lot better. She walked forward. The subway grew clearer and clearer as she walked. For a while, all she saw was the walls that were filled with graffiti and the drink vendor beside a bench. She walked a bit more and jumped.

"Toot toot!" The subway train swiped past in front of her face. She backed away just to make sure no other trains were coming. Instantly, after turning around for the entrance, she sprang up once more. For right ahead of her was the face of Ted Bart.

"AAAARRRRGGGGHHHH!" Leila howled as she rushed up the subway stairs. Ted dashed up to her. She was captured. But no, the adventure wasn't over yet.

For Robert kept looking around glumly for a sign of Ted. If he knew where Leila was, then he would be rushing up to her that very moment. Abruptly, he heard Leila screaming out for help. He listened a bit more closely.

"This is it!" he cried. "We can do the mission together!"

He headed towards Leila. It was coming from beside the jungle. He dashed inside. He wondered whether it was Ted doing this. Then he heard the sound coming nearer. Finally, it was just on top of him. It was the tree house. Robert swiftly climbed up and opened the door.

Leila was tied to the wall with vines. Ted Bart was lying down on his big, green bed, snoring loudly.

"Oh, thank goodness you're here," Leila whispered with a hint of guilt, "I'm so, so sorry, Robby.

I didn't think of what I was doing. I was so focused on the mission that we went apart."

Robert smiled and said softly, "Apology accepted. Now let's get outta here."

Robert tried pulling out the vines from Leila, but it was secured. He tried pushing it. Nope, it wasn't a better idea. He just secured it even more. He sat down on the green floor and thought and thought. Leila thought too. At the very same time, their heads lit up with a *very* different idea.

"Robby," Leila commanded, "I've got an idea. Do you have a cutter?"

Robert shook his head. Leila groaned. Robert looked around and his eyes fell on the table. A red cutter was just on top of it. He quickly grabbed it and gave it to Leila, who grinned and slashed away the vines. The vines dropped down onto the floor and wriggled.

Robert and Leila rubbed their eyes. They squinted and rubbed again. Were the vines actually moving? One of the vines grew longer. It wiggled and jiggled. A hole emerged in the middle of a sort of face, then it grew a tongue, a long red tongue that was parted at the bottom. Razor-sharp fangs sprouted on the roof of the hole. Observant, red eyes popped out in the mouth. It grew fatter and even longer.

It was a snake.

Robert and Leila screamed softly. They ran out of the tree house with the snake slithering up to them. The spies swiftly climbed down the staircase. They looked up. The snake wasn't climbing down the ladder. The both of them wiped sweat from their foreheads and sighed gladly. They looked up again, but the snake wasn't there. It was sliding down the spiral staircase. This time, Robert and Leila howled out loud. They sprinted right out of the jungle in front of a few buildings. They pushed through long, hanging vines and moved aside to not hit the trees.

"That was close," Robert said, gasping for breath.

"I'm pretty sure Ted Bart's powers are controlling plants. He must've used his powers to make the vine turn into a snake," Leila explained, pulling out her small, violet notebook. She typed what Ted's powers were.

"It says that his power is the ability to control plants and herbs. He can create patterns with them, command where they go, make them grow faster, and turn them into animals," Leila read while pointing on the screen.

After a short pause, the feeling of catching Ted turned into a thought about Franchesca.

"What do you reckon Franchesca's doing in the jungle?"

"Um, probably she went there long ago and left the spy gadget."

"Yeah, you *might* be correct, but I have a slight feeling that she's in here right now," Robert concluded.

"How do you know?"

"I don't. it's just a feeling, an intuition."

But Robert felt that he would go in there, to

check if Franchesca really was hidden, exploring the dense jungle; he thought that she must be finding the ladybug. But why would Franchesca assign them to that same mission if *she* would do it? Didn't the newsperson say that they must ask Ted Bart to join his mission? A hundred questions filled his curious head. They whirled inside his mind for a few seconds until he figured that he'd do something about it. He thought if Leila would disagree, then remembered about her love of being a spy. He decided to ask her.

"Leila, I've a suggestion," he asked. "Um, do you wanna go back in the jungle to check if Franchesca is there?"

"We're in the middle of a mission, Robby," she said.

"Well, if ya don't want to, I'm going by myself."

Nothing was stopping him now. He dashed into the jungle, waving back at Leila. The thoughts came back; he knew that he would meet Franchesca.

"Oh, how out-of-world he is," Leila sighed, crossing her arms.

In the jungle, Robert saw the tree house. He turned away. Then he looked around and spotted the ladybug lazily resting on a vine. *Why did Ted leave it there if he was so desperate to find it?* Robert thought in his head. He decided it was best if he carried it along. He picked it up on his palm. He placed a foot forward and heard a rustle of leaves. He turned towards the noise. It was just a heap of leaves in front of a tree. He shrugged, but he felt as if someone was following him. Instantly, just as he placed another step ahead, another crackle of leaves was heard. Robert's heart thumped against his chest. Surely, there *was* a person following. "Could it be…?" he murmured.

A brown-booted foot stepped out from behind the tree. Robert focused suspiciously at it. Another rubber boot stepped out, accompanied by a pair of sky-blue plants. The rest of the body emerged from behind. Robert recognized them at once. It was Franchesca. She wore a striped, baggy white t-shirt, and a large backpack.

"AAARRRGGGHHH!" Franchesca cried nervously. "Oh, I-it's you. Um, hello! H-How're you doing, Robert?"

Robert gaped at her disbelievingly. "What are you doing in the jungle? Why are you here? Are you finding the ladybug? I'm holding it here. If so, why did you tell *us* to do the mission?"

"Um, I, uh, now don't you mind about that." She placed her hands behind her back. "Where's Leila?"

"She's outside the jungle," Robert sighed. "She didn't want to come to check if you're here. Anyway, could you *please* tell me what you're doing here?"

"No."

"Please?"

"I said *no.*"

"C'mon, but I *want* to know!"

"Oh, fine," Franchesca placed her hands on her hips and said, "I heard that Insect Man escaped jail and wanted to find him. Long story."

"WHAT?" Robert exclaimed, outraged. "This is horrible! I've *got* to tell Leila!" He rushed out of the jungle.

Franchesca followed afterwards.

After telling her about it, Leila stared at the two of them, her eyes and mouth wide open.

She shook her head and said, "Let me get this straight. They're saying that Insect Man escaped jail and Franchesca went looking for him and that's the reason Ted Bart found a spy gadget here, then Robert became so interested and wanted to find her and he did. Now Franchesca's here. Now we have another mission. This is unbelievable," she said it all very fast and she turned to Robert. "What mission do we do first?"

Robert wasn't able to answer because he immediately cried, "THERE!" and pointed.

Ted Bart was just running straight at them. Chip and Dunston were chattering and eating bananas behind him. Leila forgot all about her question. They sped towards Ted and accidentally bumped into each other. Ted punched Robert's right elbow. As Leila charged towards Ted, he ducked as swiftly as he could. Robert dashed out of the way as Chip came crawling up to him impishly.

Leila removed her bonnet and placed it back in her leggings. She got a pencil case tucked into her leggings. "Robert, Chip, get outta the way!" she screamed urgently.

BOOM!

The pencil case exploded, spreading bits of its pieces all over the ground. Ted put his hands over his head to take cover as Robert and Leila laughed.

"That'll teach you a lesson," Franchesca chuckled.

Ted just placed his hands on his hips and turned away from them.

"Well, at least I don't have to get to jail," he said menacingly.

"We'll see about that," Leila snickered.

"Whaddaya mean?" Ted asked suspiciously.

"This is what we mean," Franchesca said, pulling out handcuffs from her backpack.

Ted sighed bitterly as Robert and Leila fastened the handcuffs in his hands.

The pencil case exploded, spreading bits of its pieces all over the ground.

They brought him to the police station, but the police officers didn't understand why he was so bad.

Leila brought out her notebook and explained to them, "According to my research, Ted Bart stole from banks and houses. He even killed about three Brookinos. In addition, he is the friend of the infamous Insect Man."

"Ah, okay, I understand," a police officer said.

"Sige, salamat," the police said.

Robert, Leila, and Franchesca walked out of the police station.

"I'll leave you two here," Franchesca said, trotting to the Studio. Robert and Leila went home; they forgot that they had *another* important mission.

# CHAPTER 10

## INSECT MAN'S ESCAPE

**T**he following day, Leila met Robert walking his golden retriever, Lucky, in the Brinderbrook Park. Lucky was an adult dog who had beautiful, golden fur and wore a blue collar with his name written on it.

Leila went there in a rush. The moment she woke up, she remembered about the second mission.

"Don't you remember, Robby?" Leila cried.

Robert didn't think this was a great way of greeting. "Remember what?" he asked as Lucky whirled around his feet.

"The second mission!" Leila exclaimed, throwing her arms forward. "Don't you remember? Franchesca told you that Insect Man escaped jail again and you told me crucially and we wanted to find him. The problem was that we got carried away because Ted Bart showed up and, well…"

Robert kept walking Lucky.

"Slow down, Leila," he said.

"Really, Robby," said Leila coldly. "Why can't

you understand?"

"Yes," Robert agreed politely. "I can't understand."

He continued walking without taking any notice of Leila trembling with rage.

"B-But Insect Man's a villain! You're going to help me with this mission, Robby, whether you like it or not."

"LEILA!" Robert cried, infuriated. "OF COURSE, YOU KNOW THAT I WANNA DO THIS MISSION! BUT DON'T THE MISSIONS MAKE YOU FRUSTRATED? *I AM* BECAUSE YOU KNOW HOW MUCH *I* TRAIN! WELL, YOU PROBABLY JUST WANNA BECOME THIS PROFESSIONAL SPY, DON'T YOU?"

"IT'S NOT LIKE THAT!" Leila roared.

They completely forgot that seventy-four Brookinos were standing, playing, or having a picnic in the park. The spies' anger just burst out of them like lava flowing down a volcano. The people stared at the two, turning their heads at the one shouting. Robert and Leila didn't mind.

"WHY, YES IT IS!" Robert boomed madly.

"FINE!" Leila impatiently shrieked. "FINE! I'LL DO IT ON MY OWN, THEN!"

The people began murmuring to each other as Leila stomped off. Robert didn't realize what he'd been doing. He shook his head and whispered, "This is the first time I ever fought with Leila in front of a lot of people. It doesn't matter if it's a lot of people. I wonder why I did that." He scratched Lucky behind the ears and walked him towards the exit.

When he went home, his mother walked up to him from the kitchen. Mrs. Rockedeer was a calm person with her hair tied up in a bun. She wore an orange apron, and she was still holding a frying pan.

Lucky panted as he went up a pillow beside an armchair.

"Robert," Mrs. Rockedeer asked as she wiped sweat off Robert's forehead. "I heard some noise coming from the park. It sounded as though you and Leila were having a fight."

Robert slumped himself down to an armchair but didn't reply. His mother smiled a consoling smile.

"Well," she said. She fetched a sampaguita from a pocket of her apron and placed it into Robert's hand. "It's a good luck charm."

Robert just nodded.

She brushed hair off Robert's forehead and kissed it. "You're old enough to decide what to do," she said as she walked back into the kitchen.

Robert still didn't say anything. He still felt anger in his mind, but his spirits rose up as he thought of what his mother said. He *could* do this. Just as he rose from his chair, the doorbell rang. *Let's hope it isn't Leila*, he thought as he patted Lucky.

Robert opened the door. It was his father, Mr. Rockedeer. He was wearing a necktie and he looked strong but kind. He was carrying a food delivery. He ruffled Robert's hair and said, "Busy morning?"

"A bit."

"I'm home, Ellen!" he cried to Mrs. Rockedeer.

"Yes, Harold, I heard," Mrs. Rockedeer said.

Robert bid farewell to his parents and Lucky as he walked to Leila's home. He rang the doorbell of Leila's white door. A plump lady opened it. She was holding a dustpan and her face was covered in dust and sweat. She seemed to be a helper.

"Um," Robert started.

"If you're looking for Leila then she's not here," the lady said crossly in a high-pitched tone, and she slammed the door on his face.

*She's not here?* he thought anxiously.

Robert dashed towards the Spy Studio. "She must be there, I'm sure."

He went in. Leila was climbing the Climbing Triangle with an exasperated look. She was wearing a sando and shorts. Robert took a deep breath and walked to it. He tried to get Leila's attention by jumping up and down, waving his hands in the air, and saying, "Leila? I wanted to tell you something." But Leila would not look at him. Robert decided there was just one thing to do…

"YOO-HOO! LEILA, I WANT YOU TO KNOW THAT I'M READY TO DO THE MISSION! ARE YOU?"

Leila climbed down the Climbing Triangle and placed her hands on her hips.

Robert tried to act casual even though he felt his temper rising.

"So," said Leila. "I've been thinking about the map that we used to find who we thought was Teddy Smart. He was really Ted Bart. Ted Bart was bad, but the map found him. Which means that we can use it for Insect Man. I'm right, right?"

"Yes," Robert agreed.

"Now we just need to ask for the map."

"Don't *you* have the map?"

"Oh."

Leila pulled the map out of her bag, which was hanging on one of the monkey bars, and said to it, "Where can we find Brookino villain Insect Man?"

The map didn't answer.

"Where can we find…"

Before Leila completed the sentence, though, Robert interrupted her.

"Leila, I remembered about the interview and wondered who Kenyon and Sam are."

"I'll see about it in Villains' Lair."

They almost forgot about the fight they had since they were absorbed in the mission. Robert rubbed his hands together as Leila repeated to the map, "Where can we find Insect Man?"

The map revealed bold letters containing the words they saw before.

'Follow the trails, and you will find
Insect Man.'

The beginning was the Spy Studio. Following it was a drawing of a man wearing a necktie and walking a dog.

Before anything else happened, Robert said, "Now see who Kenyon and Sam are."

"Okay."

Leila typed, 'Who is Kenyon, friend of Ted Bart.'

She read the screen. "'Kenyon Bradford a.k.a. Insect Man...' Wait, what?"

"Insect Man?" Robert exclaimed.

"Hmm, what about Sam then?" Leila typed it on her miniature laptop. "It says that Sam is a friend to Insect Man, too."

"Ah," said Robert, "I get it."

The two wore their uniforms and went out. They followed the trail and saw Robert's dad standing beside a trash bin while scratching Lucky the dog's fur. Leila waved to him, and he smiled.

"Hello, Robert," Mr. Rockedeer said.

"Hello," Robert replied.

When Mr. Rockedeer walked away, they looked back at the map. The next object was a blue cabriolet car parked in front of a plant. After walking to it, they saw another trash bin. They followed every item on the map: a truck, a crowd of people, the market, and a lady pushing a stroller containing a baby boy, the majestic hotel Leila went into before, a computer shop, and finally, they walked beside the shop and saw a little door on its wall.

`You have reached your destination,` the map revealed. `Go inside the door.`

The door's handle was rusty and brown. The door was dull green and whenever someone looked at it, a creepy sensation would fill their body.

Leila shuddered.

"Let's go in," Robert said boldly.

Leila nodded.

Robert held the handle. He opened it slightly; it creaked. Robert opened it a tiny bit more. He peeked inside the door. Nothing was seen. He opened it just the right height that he and Leila could get in. "You go in first," Robert suggested.

"Um, why d-don't you?" Leila asked fearfully. "You're much braver."

"Oh, okay. Just promise that you'll go in after me."

Robert took another peep inside. He felt a blood-curdling feeling and didn't have the slightest idea why the door or the room did that.

*Why is it so scary?* he thought.

They walked beside the shop and saw a little door on its wall.

He plucked up the courage and placed a step forward. His foot didn't touch the ground. In fact, it didn't touch anything at all. Robert placed it a bit farther, maybe a bit *too* far. He leaned and lost his balance.

"AAAARRRRGGGGHHHH!" he cried.

Then he fell with a thud. It was all pitch black. Not a single thing was to be seen, not even a bright colored insect. But that didn't fool Robert into getting frightened.

"Leila!" he screamed. "You can come down now!"

Leila took a deep breath and jumped. "Aray!" she exclaimed as she fell down to the hard floor.

They both felt their hairs stand up on the back of their necks. They tried finding each other but it was no use; they simply couldn't see. It was as if their eyes were shut tight and no light was anywhere. Robert was opening his eyes wide to try and hold Leila, but where was she?

"Hey, what about using light from the legendary Light Bonnet? Huh?" Leila proudly suggested.

"Great idea, but I'm not sure if it's legendary."

Leila tried to find her bonnet inside her uniform. "I'm sure it's in here somewhere." She dug into her boots, her hair, and everything else until she remembered that she left it in the Studio.

"Now we won't be able to see *anything*!" she wailed.

Robert gazed up on top of him. Immediately, he thought of a plan.

"I've a plan," he announced. "We will go farther."

"That's your whole plan?" Leila asked.

"Yep, we walk farther and we find light."

"You can't be sure."

"I'm only guessing." He walked, arms stretching out. "You coming or not?"

Leila groaned and followed his voice.

Robert kept saying, "Getting closer..." The both of them kept walking. They bumped on rough things several times, but they still kept wandering around the dingy room.

As Robert led Leila somewhere he thought had light, he seemed to be right. The room began to become less inky. As they moved a bit forward, it became just a bit gray. They remained moving forward, and the light became more vivid every step. At last, the room was lit.

The room was towering. It was sandy in color. A giant lamp hung on the very top. At the far side, a large dinner table was standing. Beside the wall was a row of knights wearing their metal armor, all motionless and steady. There was a door standing with a little coffee table at the other wall. Robert moved slightly closer to it. It swung open. He ducked under the coffee table. Leila edged behind one of the knights.

A man with yellow hair walked out. He was wearing a black domino mask. He wore a green colored jumper, black boots, and his smile looked unpleasantly vile.

Robert and Leila gasped.

Insect Man paced a few steps along the room.

The room was very towering. It was sandy in color. A giant, diamond chandelier hung on the very top. At the far side, a large dinner table was standing. Beside the wall was a row of knights wearing their metal protection; all motionless and steady. There was a door standing with a little coffee table at the other wall. Robert moved slightly closer to it. It swung open. He ducked under the coffee table. Leila edged behind one of the knights. They both peeped to see who was there.

A man with spiky yellow hair walked out. He was wearing a black domino mask. He wore a green colored jumper, black boots, and his smile looked unpleasantly vile.

Robert and Leila gasped.

Insect Man paced a few steps along the room. He stared darkly at the knights and turned away from them. Then he vanished. Instead, a bear appeared. It sniffed the air. Insect Man turned back into a normal person.

"I smell two little children," he said menacingly.

Robert's heart thumped faster than ever, and Leila felt sweat trickling down her back. Insect Man cackled softly and knelt beside the exact knight Leila was behind.

Leila tried to breathe quietly and covered her mouth and nose with both her hands. Insect Man jumped in, and Leila shrieked. He began chasing her all over the room. Accidentally, Leila knocked over the table Robert was under.

"Oops," she muttered guiltily, still running.

Insect Man took no attention to him.

Robert crawled to the darkness and gestured to Leila to follow. He hoped he saw her. She didn't. Robert went closer to the light and motioned again, this time Leila was nodding and rushing to the blackness. Insect Man followed. As they ran, Insect Man yelped in pain, fortuitously banging on the rugged objects.

"I wonder how Insect Man got there. Do you think he even got *scared* of the door?" Leila said curiously.

"Oh, wait. I've just remembered about a tiny flashlight in here." He fetched a jet-black flashlight from his wrist; it was hidden from his gloves.

"Ugh, you should've got that a while ago."

The two spies went back in. Robert turned on the light, but everything was absolutely pitch black. Robert bewilderedly tried clicking it open again, but everything was still as dingy as before.

"Did you forget to charge it?" Leila asked anxiously.

"I did just last night."

"Insect Man must've put some sort of spell or something."

"Let's concentrate. We followed each other's words a while ago and it worked. The trouble right now is, he made the uneven things vanish, which makes the room empty and causes our voices to echo, which means we won't really know where each other are. See?" Robert said, his voice echoing around the room. "Everything's empty."

"Let's try to…um…"

"Who's there?" said a strong and rough voice of a man.

It repeated all over the room.

"No one!" shouted Robert. The room mimicked what he said.

"If you *are* no one then who's talking?" the voice sniggered.

Leila imitated the sound of a ghost. "WOOOOOOO! Follow me, Robert."

"WOOOOOOOOOOOOOO!" they boomed in unison. Their shouts echoed around the room, and it sounded as though a hundred ghosts were there.

"AAAARRRRGGGGHHHH!" the man roared. They heard the sound of running footsteps leading to the lit room.

"Let's go there, too," Robert murmured.

They walked towards the illuminated room.

As they entered, the spies noticed two other men, aside from Insect Man. The first was wearing a long and black-hooded cloak. The man had a scepter in his hand that had a bright, glowing sphere that peculiarly glowed even when it was bright. It looked as if whoever held it would get a splinter. A lengthy white beard was tucked in his cloak. The next chap was sitting down on a chair, shivering slightly. His face looked horror-stricken.

The first man with the long beard rubbed his hands together and said to Insect Man in a silky voice, "I wonder why some sort of creatures are inside your hideout, Kenyon."

"Yes, Ejeem, I know," Insect Man said, sounding a bit anxious.

Robert and Leila were taken aback. They hardly ever thought that Insect Man would speak in a calm and scared sort of voice. All they ever heard him say were things like, "You sickening spies!"

"Well, then it mustn't be true."

"What do you mean?"

"I mean about those two," Ejeem said, pointing his finger at the spies.

"Erm, kumusta?" Robert greeted apprehensively.

The things they heard were, "GET THOSE TWO SICKENING SPIES!" and "I'M GONNA GET YOU!"

The two spies went back to the room with knights. The shivering male was still there.

"AREN'T YOU THOSE KIDS THAT PHIL TALKED ABOUT?" he cried in a rough voice. It was the man they had scared.

Leila put on some earbuds. They detected the person talking, who he was, and if he was evil or not.

"What?" Robert asked.

"I SAID, AREN'T YOU THOSE KIDS THAT PHIL TALKED ABOUT!" the man repeated.

"Detecting, detecting..." Leila's earbuds said. "Found. Found. He is Sam Ferbee, evil."

"Ah, hello, Sam," she whispered cunningly.

"Um, yeah, hello, Sam," Robert said, stuttering a bit.

"Hello!" Sam said.

Robert walked towards her, and they both turned to Sam. But he wasn't there on the chair. As a matter of fact, he wasn't anywhere in the room! Leila searched behind the knights while Robert turned over the coffee table. As he stood the table up again, he accidentally glanced at the door that Insect Man went in with. He wondered where it led to. *Hmm*, he thought, *maybe it leads to a secret laboratory, or maybe an indoor forest?*

"Leila," he suggested. "Could we just check what's in this door for a while?"

Leila didn't answer. She stopped checking behind the knights and knocked them over instead. Robert repeated it a bit louder, but Leila was so concentrated that Robert's voice wasn't audible to her.

He decided that he could do it on his own. He thought that maybe he'd just look at a bit of it. What could be wrong? He walked to the door and opened it slightly. He peeped inside and saw a little blue, watery thing. He opened it a bit more. He saw waves inside a sort of sphere. Now, he went in and saw a giant sphere floating in the air. He immediately felt that this was not the right place to be in and knew that there was somebody watching, whoever it was. He went back out, slammed the door shut, and told Leila, "Maybe Sam's in the dark spot."

"We won't be able to see him if it's so dark."

"What about the scepter that we saw glow even here?"

The spies walked into the inky room and tried spotting anything that was glowing bright. They looked and looked. Instantly, Robert saw something bright at the edge.

"There," Robert muttered. His voice sounded a tiny bit loud in the silence.

"Where?" Leila whispered.

"Over there," he murmured.

"Why are we whispering?" she asked.

"I have no idea," he shrugged.

They tried to get to the light. It was much easier now that Insect Man removed all the objects blocking the way. Finally, they reached it. They saw a wrinkled, old face hidden in a cloak.

"Kenyon?" Ejeem said. "Sam, where's Kenyon?"

"I don't know," Sam, who was beside Ejeem, answered.

"Insect Man's not here?" the spies said in unison.

They extended their arms once again and walked to the door. A few times, they bumped into the walls and lost each other, but they both reached the door together.

In front of the shop, Robert and Leila saw a glimpse of yellow racing down the street. They endeavored with all their speed to catch up with Insect Man as quickly as possible. Abruptly, Insect Man vanished. Instead, a large, spotted cat with long, thin legs and a long tail sped along the street.

"What animal did Insect Man turn into?" Robert

asked behind the gushing wind.

"A cheetah!" Leila cried, her hair blowing in her face.

"We should try to be faster if we wanna catch a cheetah!" Robert said.

The cheetah dashed swiftly into the Green Jungle. Robert and Leila darted past the vines and leaves and sprinted after Insect Man. They saw his long tail run through a bunch of hanging vines and disappear.

The spies pushed away the vines and reached a deserted land of sand, all scorching hot. They saw Insect Man shape-shift back into a man and walk to a group of people wearing large, thick sweaters even in the blazing weather. On the other side, they saw Ivory Lark relaxing on a wooden bench. Behind Ivory was Philippe Gorly-Borly doing push-ups. There were some other people talking to each other and exercising.

Robert and Leila felt something violent in the air. The sky turned musty, and a gush of wind blew over them.

"Great," they chorused, sighing.

# CHAPTER 11

## THE ULTIMATE BATTLE

Robert and Leila's walking ceased. Everyone stared at the spies as they stared at the people, who turned out to be villains. The duo smiled weakly.

"Hello?" Robert said.

"AAAARRRRGGGGHHHH!" all the villains boomed angrily. They headed to the spies.

Rushing behind a giant rock, Robert and Leila crouched.

Leila put on some earbuds that weren't the ones before, pressed on it, and muttered urgently, "This is Leila. Robert and I found Insect Man, and now he and other villains are starting some sort of battle. We're somewhere near the Green Jungle in a sandy place. Please come quick. I repeat, please come quick."

"Who'd you talk to?"

"Franchesca."

Robert nodded and crawled out of the back of the huge rock. Leila tugged on his uniform and said under her breath, "Where are you going?"

"To the battle, of course."

"Are you insane?"

He ignored her and continued crawling.

When he was in front of the rock, Leila followed after.

Robert was holding a laser pen on his right hand and a triangular shield on his left. Leila reluctantly got her ear buds that recognized who was talking.

Ivory headed straight to Robert. Her chestnut hair blew in the wind, and the wound on her right arm looked as if it glowed in the scorching weather.

She cackled, "Ah, if it isn't the boy who stole my Monkey."

"I did not steal *your* Monkey," Robert said bitterly.

"Well then, you seized it from me," she said and pulled out a sword from her back, darted to Robert as he ducked and twirled. He jumped when Ivory's sword slashed under him.

"I never knew you were a dancer," Ivory laughed.

Robert shook in fury and dashed to her. He kicked her left arm and punched her right.

"Yow!" she exclaimed in pain.

Robert didn't feel sorry.

"What did you do…?" Ivory muffled.

"I believe that I just punched and kicked you," he said angrily.

On the other hand, Leila was back behind the rock. She was too frightened about what might happen. Then, without warning, an army of people in black dashed out of the jungle. Hidden in the midst of all, Franchesca was running. She met Franchesca's eyes, and Franchesca winked.

"Robby, they're here!" Leila cried eagerly.

"Who's here?" Robert asked through the active moves of Ivory's sword.

Leila didn't need to answer. The spies that Franchesca brought each rushed to their own bad guys and began fighting.

"I didn't mean you bring all the spies you find," Leila said to Franchesca in disbelief and awe.

"The more the merrier," Franchesca said, blasting some bombs.

Robert saw a glimpse of someone that looked familiar. He tilted his head to one side and realized it was Mr. Ramos, his teacher in Brinderbrook Academy. He saw Leila, who was setting the timer of her exploding pencil case.

"Robby," she whispered. "When you hear a high-pitched noise, hide behind something—GET OUT OF THE WAY!"

Insect Man turned into an elephant and blew his trunk. A mighty gust of wind darted out of it. Insect Man became human again and strutted towards them.

"Not that strong, are you?" he said.

"Oh, we'll see about that," Robert said, speeding towards him. He attempted to punch him, but Insect Man shape-shifted into an eagle and flew above them.

"Not that fast either," Insect Man laughed.

Leila borrowed a balloon that wasn't blown yet from a funny-looking spy. She blew it and held it up, directly to Insect Man. She let go. The balloon whirled around the air for a few seconds and hit Insect Man hard on the top of his beak. He turned back into a person, fell to the sand, and rubbed his nose.

"How 'bout that?" Leila said proudly.

Insect Man said nothing and punched Robert in the stomach.

"OW!" Robert exclaimed.

As they fought, they heard a high-pitched noise. At first, they didn't know what it was, then realized it was the pencil-case and ran.

After hiding behind a large rock, they heard a large explosion.

BOOM!

The pencil case detonated to bits. Insect Man, who was very close to the pencil-case, shielded himself with wings as he transformed into a giant vulture. A scared-looking spy ran for his life. Robert and Leila pressed their hands on their ears due to the deafening sound the explosion gave.

Robert and Leila decided to ask Insect Man the question that they thought of on their third mission.

"This is an important question," Robert began, "Why does Insect Man wanna steal Maria Senabi, the Golden Monkey, and the unique lady bug?"

"Now you can't just think that I'll answer that question, do you, boy?" Insect Man roared while shape-shifting into a cheetah. "You can't catch me!"

he purred slyly.

"Oh, I'm sure we can," Leila whispered.

"We've done it before," said Robert.

The spies sprinted swiftly towards Insect Man, who was heading towards the jungle. They saw him growl angrily to something close to a tree. The duo shoved aside the same hanging vines that always block the way and saw Insect Man get nearer and nearer.

"Why do you think he's stealing those things?" Robert questioned while panting a bit.

"D'know," Leila shrugged. While running, she looked at the tree Insect Man growled at. "Hey, isn't that Lucky?"

"What's lucky? I think we're not getting any luck right now. Insect Man's still..."

"Your dog."

"Insect Man isn't my dog," Robert said, befuddled.

"No. I can see Lucky, your golden retriever, beside the tree in front of you."

Robert looked and saw his dog smiling at him. He stopped panting and grinned.

"Now," he said. "I wonder why you're here, Lucky."

Lucky barked. He pulled out a piece of paper from his collar. Robert got it from him.

"It says," he said. "It says, 'I gave this to your dog because I need your help. Turn this over.'" He flipped the paper and read, 'Go in the door beside the shop, go into the door with the spherical water orb, and wait for me.' Is he or she talking about Insect Man's lair or something? Why does this person need help? And we don't know who he or she is."

"Yeah, let's do this thing later," Leila said quickly. "We should have business with Insect Man first." And she followed the tracks of Insect Man.

"But..." He groaned. "C'mon, Lucky."

They walked past trees and bushes, past squishy mud and foul insects, through hanging jungle vines (Robert tried swinging on one) and enormous trees, until they saw a clear silhouette of Insect Man.

Robert and Leila dashed to him as he hopped over a puddle of mud. Luckily, Insect Man's foot got tangled in a pile of vines. "Yes!" they cried as Insect Man groaned. The spies grabbed his arms as Lucky held his pants with his mouth, and they began to drag him all the way to the sandy land.

Everyone was battling. They were kicking and punching, fencing and wrestling, until...

"Lucky!" Robert cried, trying to calm him down. "Whoa, boy! What's going on?"

Lucky barked and turned his head to the left. Robert and Leila followed. An old person on a wheel chair was there, turning the wheels round to get closer.

"You haven't got my letter, dearie?" he wheezed.

"What? I, uh, I did get a letter..." Robert stammered.

"Oh, that's alright. But I was just wondering if you'd like to hear why Insect Man was doing all these horrible deeds. That's exactly why I called you."

Robert looked at him. "Sorry, I didn't understand."

"Your dog told me he heard you whispering something about knowing what Insect Man was up to."

"Lucky," Robert said, turning to the dog. "How did you…?"

Lucky barked and wagged his tail.

"I can interpret what dogs say. For example, your dog just said that he agrees with me."

"Wow…"

"So, would you like to hear it?"

Robert looked at Leila, who shrugged then nodded swiftly. Robert nodded back and looked at Insect Man, who was shaking his head quickly as if telling the old man to stop talking. So, Robert thought he'd agree.

"Yes, sure."

The elderly man grinned and said, "Okay. First, I need to ask permission to Insect Man."

"WHAT?" Robert exclaimed disbelievingly.

"Oh, fine. I believe no harm would be done if I just told you."

The villains and spies were listening intently and probably forgetting about the fight.

Insect Man sat motionless, except that Robert and Leila heard him give a little angry squeak.

"Let me begin," the man started. Insect Man covered his ears in a cross sort of way and looked like he was going to stand up and tell the man to be quiet, but he wasn't able to move.

"Okay, so, it all started when the teenage Insect Man found me beside an overflowing trash bin. I was like an indigent stray dog finally finding an owner. The difference is that I am not a dog. You see, I was a very poor Brookino when I was young. I lived near trash and garbage, studied through newspapers, ate with scraps, begged, you know. And I was absolutely ill at the time 'til now.

"No one knew what my sickness was, and the mayor even tried helping, and many passersby felt sorry for me and offered me different sorts of delicious food, but I was not feeling better at all, except for the fact I had food to eat.

"Anyway, one of the passersby was the young Kenyon. He told me to stand up and follow him. That moment, I felt that something good was about to happen. You know that feeling, when someone invites you and you feel that he's going to be your friend. When you find a poor cat and you feel that it would be your pet…

"Sorry, got a little carried away there. Anyway, he's really a calm little fellow before. And he brought me to his home and invited me for a cup of tea."

"Insect Man didn't start badly?" Robert asked in disbelief.

"Oh, yes," the gray-haired man replied, nodding quickly. "He was a very good chap back then. Once, I even saw him help an elderly lady cross the busy street. I remember looking at him donating some money to the poor, too."

At that, Robert and Leila kept quiet. The whole crowd gathered.

"As some years passed by," the wheelchaired man carried on, "Insect Man grew into an adult like now. I lived with him almost my entire life. We did everything together. Even though I'm much older, it felt as if Kenyon was my father, and friend, and he took care of me. We were such good friends that Insect Man wanted to find a cure to my illness. I thanked him gratefully." He smiled at Insect Man, who was trembling with fury.

"And finally, I'll begin the secret. Insect Man was so desperate to find a cure that he became bad. I have no idea why, but I let him be." ("How could you!" Franchesca whispered angrily.) "I guess all he wanted was to find me something good.

"As days flowed into months, he almost stole everything he could find that would make me happy. You wondered why he tried stealing the Golden Monkey, right. He wanted to steal it because it has incredible powers to give people extra strength. And I was very weak. But you and that girl over there"—he indicated Leila—"got it from him, I mean Ivory. The Golden Monkey has incredible powers to bring back your strength or even give you some.

And so, he thought of the famous movie Spy Women. Maria Senabi, actress of the protagonist, was his target. He wanted her to entertain me so he told his friend Philippe Gorly-Borly to capture her. I let him be, and, well, I don't know why, but I was sure I should stop him, but I couldn't, or I wouldn't…

"Ahh, I don't know. Once again, the both of you saved her. After, he wanted the ladybug. Ted Bart disguised himself as Teddy Smart and discovered a ladybug with a thousand polka-dots. So, there is no such thing as a man called Teddy Smart, but a villain called Ted. Ted told Insect Man that he inspected the lady bug and saw that it can heal the eater of any sickness. And, repeated all over again, you did it.

"Insect Man was furious and wanted to think of the greatest plan he's ever had. So, he gathered every friend, foe, and followers with him in this place. Then the two of you came and blah, blah, blah, you know what happened. So that's all. By the way, that water sphere you saw was where Kenyon thought of keeping the things he'd steal, but he stole nothing.

"And, if you'd like to know, your dog just sniffed the trail of your footsteps to find me. You see, I called for him with a howl. In addition, Kenyon placed a curse on his hideout's door, and that's the reason it made you frightened."

A few of the crowd were muttering something. A third of them were crying and wiping their eyes frantically. Another of them, who were villains, gazed at the man and roared ballistically. A group of spies were hugging each other as if they never wanted to be separated. Maria and Francesca's looks were half awed and half angry.

Insect Man was the only one who was angriest as ever.

"Let me get this straight," Leila said, finding her voice. "Insect Man wasn't really a villain when he was young, and he just turned into one to *help* you. That means he cared for you even though it seems like…"

Insect Man cut her off.

"ENOUGH," he bellowed. The whisperers stopped whispering. The spies seemingly stopped hugging. The miserable cryers wiped away their tears. The villains rubbed their eyes to stop the staring.

Insect Man clasped his hands together, narrowed his eyebrows to make him look scarier and angrier than ever, and pointed into the jungle.

"OUT!" he exploded. "*Everybody*!"

The villains nodded uneasily and followed.

"I said *everybody*," Insect Man roared.

"We won't follow you," a confident but wheezy voice said bravely.

"I agree with Fred," said a dreamy, girlish voice through the hugging group of spies.

"Me, too."

"Me, three."

Unfortunately, before Robert and Leila could do something, Insect Man swiftly shape-shifted into a golden, mighty creature that they did not recognize. It was almost bird-like, with a beak, except it had a sort of fish tail and a fin on its back. It had pearly white talons, as if they were carved by an expert. Its wings were extremely huge and bat-like. It had long, razor-sharp fangs that looked as if they would tear your entire body apart. Insect Man blew a shivering, chilly blow at Robert and Leila.

"What's that for?" Leila roared, quivering

slightly.

Insect Man couldn't speak. Instead, he made an ear-piercing, blood-curdling scream that sounded like a banshee.

Everyone covered their ears and backed away.

"What animal are you, Insect Man?" Robert asked crossly.

In response, Insect Man bitterly made the banshee-like scream again.

"I think he's a Hoduchde," Leila screamed. She said it like this. Ho-duke-de.

"What's a Hoduck-whatever?" questioned Robert.

"It's a mythical Brookino creature and whoever mistakenly shape-shifts into it will only be able to turn back into normal after one whole day. Shape-shifters turn into it when they can't control they're powers any longer and feel like they wanna become a dangerous creature."

"You're telling me that Insect Man can turn into non-existent animals?" Robert asked.

"I think so…"

"And Insect Man turned into a Ho-something by accident?"

"Maybe…"

"Insect Man can't be brought to jail as a giant animal."

"I know, but the police station has a giant jail."

Insect Man the Hoduchde slashed his tail on Robert's foot. He blew the chilly blow to Leila.

Once more, Insect Man's blood-curdling

screech filled the air. Insect Man screeched again and, with one humongous swipe of a talon, he tore away a tree, and it dropped down on the rock that Robert and Leila hid behind a while ago. He kicked it to the crowd of spies. It rolled and rolled. Robert tried pulling it away and Leila tried pushing it, but it continued rolling on. It slammed on the talkative boy called Fred. Fred began wailing out loud and crying his eyes out as Maria carried him towards a large, smooth stone.

"We need a plan," Robert said importantly.

"Yes, but we must do it quickly," said Leila.

"Okay, tell me about the H-o-something."

"You mean Hoduchde. I told you about it a while ago," Leila explained swiftly. "In addition, its weaknesses are people scratching behind its ears, well, of course, dying, and last but not the least, it hates its feet getting tickled. The problem is, we don't know how to get him tickled."

"Feathers, maybe," a girl suggested from the listening audience of spies.

"Thanks," Leila agreed. "Trouble's where can we find feathers?"

"I've got some," Fred pointed out weakly. He revealed a bag of feathers.

"Okay. But why are you bringing feathers?"

"It's Prank Day in my school, and I did this tickling act to all my classmates, about thirty or fifty, or sixty?"

"Everyone," Robert ordered as Insect Man watched angrily. "Everyone, get a feather and tickle the Hodirled's right foot."

"Hoduchde," Leila corrected him.

About twenty spies pulled out twenty feathers and brushed Insect Man's foot with it.

Nothing happened. Insect Man didn't laugh or anything. Immediately, he slashed his talons and stomped that all the spies tickling him fell down. Others hauled them back up.

The two spies almost forgot that Lucky and the old man were there. They didn't go out into the jungle. Instantly, Robert thought of a plan.

"Lucky and sir," he started. "Could you help us here?"

Then he turned to everybody, "Why don't we *all* work together? Besides, *just* tickling doesn't work. What about if we scratch his ear *and* tickle his foot? As Leila pointed out, we shouldn't kill him. So, who's with me? I mean, who's with *us*?"

"ME!"

"Me?"

"I am!"

"Me, too!"

"WE ARE!" everyone said in unison.

Leila roared dramatically. "Let's do it!"

Half of the spies got their own feathers (Fred's feathers seemed to be a *lot*) and began tickling Insect Man's foot, as he gave a high-pitched giggling.

On the other hand, another half of the spies built a long and strong vine ladder and hung it to Insect Man's curvy cat ears. They climbed up five by five and scratched his ear. Franchesca was with the feathers and Maria was with the scratching.

Robert and Leila were both tickling Insect Man's huge foot. Lucky and the elderly man were holding the vine rope.

Insect Man shook his head, trying to get rid of the spies.

A few fell down and got hurt, but someone came to aid.

Insect Man stopped giggling, frowned, and gave the banshee-like scream one last time. He fainted.

On the other hand, another half of the spies built a long and strong vine ladder and hung it to Insect Man's curvy cat ears.

"Now," Robert said. "All we need to do is wait for him to turn back to a human, but it would take ages."

"Maybe Lucky can take guard and bark at us when he becomes human," Leila suggested.

"What if he stopped fainting?" Robert abruptly asked.

"Lucky can bite him, maybe."

"Okay, it's settled," Franchesca announced to all the spies. "Now let's get on with the other villains. I was wondering where they are."

"I think I know," said Leila. Letting Lucky take watch, she led them to Ted's treehouse, where there was indistinct muttering.

Robert, Leila, and Franchesca walked up the spiral staircase and heard all the villains talking about Insect Man.

"Why do you think he let us out?" one asked.

"Maybe he wanted to have his own time alone with the pesky spies."

"Yeah, but what if he just got tired of all the fighting?"

"Why don't we just go back to see what's happened?"

"Yeah, I need to find out what's happened to my best friend."

"He just might get angry with us."

Robert, Leila, and Franchesca sneakily tip-toed inside and hid under the table with bananas. As a curly-topped villain got a banana, they crawled away from under it and went back-to-back with the wall.

"On the count of three," Leila said. "We capture them with handcuffs."

"We need much more spies for many villains,"

Franchesca breathed.

"Then," Robert said. "Let's go and tell them."

Leila creeped back to the door and announced softly, "We need all of you to go there." She indicated windows at the sides of Ted's treehouse. "And when we say three, we place handcuffs on the villains. I think you guys have those with you, right?"

Everyone nodded and followed.

In the treehouse, as Leila went in, the villains were chattering happily about something else.

"Ready?" Franchesca asked.

"One," Robert started.

"Two," Leila said.

"THREE!" the two chorused.

All the spies went in through the windows and secured the handcuffs on the villains.

Robert did it on Ivory. Leila fastened the handcuffs to Philippe.

Maria did it swiftly to Ted as Franchesca made someone lay flat on the ground as she secured the cuffs.

All the villains groaned grimly. They couldn't stand up because all the spies were pushing them down. Pulling the villains with them, the members of the Spy Studio heard Lucky bark. Robert and Leila looked bewilderedly at each other. The sun wasn't even setting, but Insect Man's turned into a human *already*?

They all ran into the sandy land and saw Lucky biting Insect Man's leg. Insect Man already *did* become a human.

Leila put her hand on her forehead and exclaimed, "I remember! A dog's bite can also turn a Hoduchde into a human again! It's one thing that can make them turn into normal!"

"Lucky," Robert asked. "Did Insect Man stop fainting a while ago?"

Lucky barked and panted.

Robert put his hand up, and Lucky high-fived it.

Insect Man fainted again. He looked too tired to even stand up. All the villains looked at him, horrified.

Franchesca declared, "I want all of you to bring those villains to the police station. Robert, Leila, the both of you'll tell the policemen to take close watch in case they escape *and* that the jails should be secure."

"Why should we get to jail if you didn't even go into the jungle?" a villain asked.

"Because you're bad, and we're good," Fred laughed.

Robert and Leila fist-bombed happily and trotted towards Green Jungle.

As they led the way, all the spies followed. The villains struggled to escape, and it was no use; Franchesca and Maria's handcuffs were very strong.

Suddenly, Maria came running up to Robert and Leila.

"I've been thinking," she said. "Both of you should be the one bringing Insect Man since the both of you were the ones who saved the day."

"Brilliant," Robert exclaimed.

"With pleasure," said Leila.

Reaching the station, the policeman began a frenzy of gratitude. They bowed and handed everyone doughnuts and mugs of juice and coffee.

They shook every spy's hand one by one, when a police man asked Robert and Leila, "Do you even *know* if all these villains you captured are bad?"

"Well," Leila explained. "I put on some goggles and saw that they *are* evil."

She was meaning the Spy Studio Dawn Goggles. She secretly used them in Ted's treehouse and scanned everyone's faces. She did it swiftly because the Goggles had a button that could do things quickly, not one by one.

"Genius," the chief of the policeman gasped.

"Oh, and when they're brought to jail, please make someone that *never ever* gets bored guard the jail, and be *sure* that there are no other ways out," Robert added sternly.

"We always do," the police said. "But you've captured Insect Man, Hardest Brookino Villain to Capture, and Most Horrible Bad Guy in Brinderbrook City, et cetera."

Insect Man groaned, suddenly waking up. "I don't see the reason why I have to be the Most Horrible Bad Guy in Brinderbrook City. Can't someone else be the one?"

Robert and Leila laughed.

# CHAPTER 12

## SPIES OF THE YEAR

The following day, when Robert woke up, he heard his mother calling.

"Darling, Robert! Someone called Franchesca Birtwick is calling on the phone!"

Robert rubbed his eyes, yawned and stretched, and sat down on his bed.

*Now*, he thought. *It can't be another mission, can it?*

"COMING!" he cried, quickly walking down the steps.

His mother was cooking bacon and his father was reading the magazine. Lucky was still fast asleep beside the armchair Mr. Rockedeer was sitting on.

Robert walked to a lone chair and answered the call.

"Insect Man hasn't escaped jail once more, has he?" he asked.

"What?" Franchesca laughed. "No. I'm just telling you that after you eat your breakfast, you should go to the Spy Studio."

"Okay, as long as I won't be late for school. The principal called last night and told me I've been late for, er, the days of the missions."

"I promise that it will be as quick as a wink."

"So then get here. Clock's tickin'!"

After playing one round of fetch with Lucky and eating a plate of bacon, rice, and egg, Robert kissed his parents and said, "See you later."

"Stay safe," his mother and father told him.

Leila was waiting in front of the Studio. She was full of sweat, and her orange-brown hair was disheveled.

"I got here as quick as I can," she said, panting.

"Should we put on our uniforms?" he asked her.

"Nope, I think."

They went in and saw a large banner hung in front of the Climbing Triangle that said in heroic lettering, '**WE DEFEATED INSECT MAN! HURRAH!**' The spy gadgets Franchesca transferred in the Studio were all organized neatly on shelves.

A large, three-layered cake was on a circular table in the middle.

Abruptly, out of nowhere and to the spies' surprise, Franchesca walked towards them.

"Ivory didn't share her powers with you, did she?" Leila gasped.

"No," Franchesca said. "Just walked with the shadows. Anyway, both of you need to be here before the celebration."

"Celebration?" the spies asked in unison.

"Yes. I mean, we need a celebration for defeating and capturing the villains. Oh, look. Here comes the old man."

Indeed, the old person who told all the spies about Insect Man's story was turning his wheelchair in the Studio.

"Why did you tell him where the spies train? It also means that you told him we're spies," Leila asked seriously.

"I didn't," Franchesca muttered. "The wise man knows."

"Oh, please," the old man said, apparently hearing the conversation. "Just call me by the name Elderly and Wrinkled Old Man. I'm tired of being called 'old man' or 'wise man.'"

Instantly after they nodded, about more than thirty spies zoomed into the Studio. They were all wearing party hats, holding gifts, and screaming about Insect Man.

It seemed that the battle the previous day was still squirming in their heads. Clearly, Robert and Leila were glad that there were much more spies in the Studio than there had ever been before. It *was* a big celebration.

Franchesca presented the giant cake to everyone and yelled, "Dig in!"

The cake was scrumptious. It had chocolate filling and the bread smelled of roses. Everybody had a great time.

In addition to the food, Franchesca, Maria, and Elderly and Wrinkled Old Man set up a few games. The spy children laughed and played joyfully as the grown-ups played board games.

Robert and Leila chatted with a few other spies, with Fred, some other kids, and a teenager whom they called Henry.

After minutes of fun, the spies began saying farewells to each other and giving away presents. When only Robert, Leila, and Franchesca were left, Franchesca pulled out a neatly wrapped gift from under the monkey bars. The box was sky blue, with yellow stripes and a violet ribbon.

"For your bravery and teamwork," she said to them proudly. "I award this to both of you. Maria and I wrapped it with pride of having you as students." Then she added happily, "There are two gifts there, so just see the one with your name and one thing for the both of you to share." And she skipped out of the Spy Studio, waving goodbye.

Robert and Leila asked each other at the same time, "Should we open it here or at my house?"

"Here," they answered in unison.

"I'll untie the ribbon," Robert said.

"Sure."

Robert slowly unfastened the ribbon and placed it aside.

"I think *you* should open the lid," he said. "I'm too nervous."

"If you say so," Leila said.

She carefully put away the box's lid and gasped disbelievingly. Robert peeped in and gasped, too. It was too good to be true.

A brown framed certificate was lying in the box. The paper was yellow and looked as if it was the back of a treasure map. It said:

*To Robert and Leila, two fearless spies of the Spy Studio, I hereby award you the Spy of the Year Award. This means that you have accomplished an almost impossible task and did it courageously. This also means you have been awarded as true spies.*

*Sincerely,*
*Franchesca Birtwick*
*Leader of the Spy Studio*

Spy of the Year

On each side of the frame, a golden medal was placed, shimmering. It had a golden star carved on it and letters saying **Spy of the Year** and their names under the star.

Leila immediately got hers and placed it on her neck. She examined it carefully and gave a little squeak of extreme pleasure.

Robert got his and polished it on his clothes. It shimmered even more. He wore it just like Leila and rubbed it a bit more so that it shone as bright as a light bulb.

"Is this *real* gold?" Leila asked swiftly and eagerly.

Robert shrugged and continued polishing.

"Oh, wait," added Leila, "obviously this means we're *actual* spies now, right?"

"Franchesca wrote so," Robert said.

They walked home, the medals thumping against their chests. But before they did so, they displayed their framed certificate in the middle of Spy Studio, but Robert said that they should move it to the side so as to not cause anyone wondering why *they* were in the middle of the place.

Robert and Leila almost forgot that the following week was summer vacation. They really got carried away in all the missions.

The next week, once again, Leila saw Robert in Brinderbrook Park walking Lucky, who was trying to catch a squirrel. Leila was bringing her medal with her.

"Didn't want to leave the Spy of the Year Award at home?" Robert asked.

"Yep," Leila responded.

"Watched Mr. Brooke's News for any sign of Insect Man's pals or anything?" Robert questioned.

"I did this morning, but they just kept talking about an elephant painting a portrait of Brinderbrook's mayor."

"Oh, great," he groaned.

"Why? Still wanna have the missions?"

"You just read my mind."

"Well, of course, you wouldn't just let the missions slip out of your head, right? I mean, the missions were unforgettable adventures."

"Ah," Robert sighed. "The memories. Do you think we'll still be training in the Spy Studio?"

"Robby, it's summer vacation."

"Oh, right."

The two strolled along in the park for a few minutes as Lucky chased the squirrel.

"Hey," Robert added. "Leila, I've been thinking…"

"What?"

"Well, we're spies, so we must have a team name. Right?"

"Mhmm."

"So, what should we call ourselves?"

"Let me think." There was a short pause. "Sparkled Spies? Spies of Galore? The Spies of the Studio?"

"Okay, those are good," Robert said, then suddenly, "How 'bout we're called *Brinderbrook Spies*?"

"Nice. I like it."

# ACKNOWLEDGMENT

To God, I praise and glorify You for giving me this opportunity to be a writer at the age of ten;

To BWC and CFA, thank you for being the bridge to making my dream a reality;

To Teacher Rhoda, for teaching me at The Writers Club and encouraging me to become a great writer;

To Coach KB, for being a patient and hardworking editor;

To Ms. Cha, for your guidance during the whole process of publishing the book and for pushing me to finish the book cover;

To Ms. Naomi, for your tips and knowledge on marketing;

And most of all, to my family, for being my cheerleaders and greatest supporters.

# ABOUT THE AUTHOR

Nikita Santos is a ten-year-old student of CFA Homeschool from Tarlac City, Philippines. A big fan of the *Harry Potter* series, she gets inspiration from just about anything, may it be from books, movies, and everyday ordinary experiences. Her recent fantasy was created while playing a game of spies with her siblings. She loves drawing, painting, reading books, computer editing, stop-motion editing, and playing board games. *Brinderbook Spies* is her first published fiction.

# BOOKS AVAILABLE FROM BWC

## Book Writers Club
### BATCH 2

Brinderbrook Spies
by Nikita Santos

The Dark Princess
by Jannah Brielle Lising

One Summer
in Bert's Life
by Miguel Lorenzo

Temporarily Vanilla
by Kiersten Cheryl Abadicio

Homeschooled
in the Kitchen
by Pio Calungcaguin

Like and follow our Facebook page:
BWC Book Writers Club
www.facebook.com/bookwritersclub123